TRICK'S TRAP

A SINGULAR OBSESSION NOVEL

LUCY LEROUX

http://www.authorlucyleroux.com
ISBN: 978-1-942336-26-6
First Edition.

DISCLAIMER

TITLES BY LUCY LEROUX

Making Her His, A Singular Obsession, Book One
Available Now
Confiscating Charlie, A Free Singular Obsession Novelette
Available Now
Calen's Captive, A Singular Obsession, Book Two
Available Now
Take Me, A Singular Obsession Prequel Novella
Available Now
Stolen Angel, A Singular Obsession, Book Three
Available Now
The Roman's Woman, A Singular Obsession, Book Four
Available Now
Save Me, A Singular Obsession Novella, Book 4.5
Available Now
Trick's Trap, A Singular Obsession, Book Five
Available Now
Peyton's Price, A Singular Obsession, Book Six
Coming Soon

***

The Hex, A Free Spellbound Regency Short
Available Now
Cursed, A Spellbound Regency Novel
Available Now
Black Widow, A Spellbound Regency Novel, Book Two
Available Now
Haunted, A Spellbound Regency Novel, Book Three
Coming Soon

***

Writing As L.B. Gilbert
Discordia, A Free Elementals Prequel Short,
Available Now
Fire: The Elementals Book One
Available Now
Air: The Elementals Book Two
Available Now
Water: The Elementals Book Three
Coming Soon

Kin Selection
Available now

CREDITS

Cover Design: Robin Harper
http://www.wickedbydesigncovers.com

Editor: Cynthia Shepp
http://www.cynthiashepp.com/

Thank you to all of my readers!

CHAPTER 1

Trick Tyler glanced over his cards at the beautiful brunette sitting across from him. She wasn't just winning—she was *destroying* him.

He hadn't lost this badly in ages, not since his older brother Liam first taught him how to play poker.

Trick squinted at his cards. Three of a kind, a middling hand. He'd won with less, but his gut told him it wasn't enough. Not against this girl. There was no way to turn this around. He was going to lose.

Well, I may as well enjoy the ride down. He threw a few hundred-dollar chips on the stack in the center of the table with a flourish.

Was it his imagination or did his adversary smile? He wasn't sure. She had an incredible poker face...and an incredible everything else. Trick fixed on her full lips a beat too long before forcing his focus back to the game as she matched his bet.

Didn't work. Even her hands were amazing. *Huh.* He'd always thought long nails were elegant. Now they seemed excessive somehow compared to these neat unpainted ones.

Waxing poetic on a woman's nails? What was wrong with him? Everything about this girl was scrambling his signals.

The only other player, a sweaty middle-aged man, folded with a grunt. He shot them a dirty look before standing and heading to the bar.

Feeling decadent, Trick threw another grand in chips into the pile in the middle of the table, then peeked at the girl again. She lifted her drink to her lip, sucking it up through a tiny red straw. All the blood in his head promptly rushed south.

Trick gave himself a little shake. If he didn't end this, he was going to embarrass himself. "I call."

He held his breath, mesmerized, as his alluring adversary laid her cards on the table.

Of course. She had a straight, which beat his two pair. It was official—he'd lost.

"Will you marry me?" The words were out of his mouth without thought, but he wasn't about to take them back.

The girl stopped with her hand halfway to the chips. Trick smiled at her. One corner of her lip turned up, but he wasn't sure if she was smiling back.

She pushed her chair away from the table. "The last guy I beat wearing a suit like yours didn't propose. He accused me of cheating."

Her voice was like a warm whiskey. He immediately fell in love with the rich buttery sound.

Trick dismissed her observation about men in suits with a wave. "That guy was a jackass. What do you say to a June wedding?"

This time, she laughed. Suddenly feeling like a winner, he sat back as she signaled Chao, their host. "Can I please cash out?" she asked him when he arrived.

Damn. Did that mean she was leaving?

Chao murmured something and handed the chips to an underling. They were duly carried off to the no-go zone in the back where the count room was located. The brunette turned away.

"Are you sure you want to go without setting a date? Our children would be the most adorable sharks on the playground," he called after her.

She turned and smirked, but only for a second. Trick half-considered following her, but chasing her smacked of desperation. He hadn't chased a girl since...ever. Even in school, they chased him.

Smiling wistfully, he watched the brunette go. She banked left, heading in the direction of the bar and bathrooms.

It's not the exit...night's not over yet.

He rose to his feet, heading to the small dais where the owner's private table was located. From there, the gangster observed his domain. "Tell me everything about her, Chao."

Chao didn't bat an eyelash, but Trick sensed he was amused.

"I'm very sorry, *Mr. Scott,* but I can't oblige," Chao said with an emphasis on the name. "You understand."

Damn. Trick should have known he wouldn't get anything out of his crusty host. Chao knew his name wasn't Scott. One of the reasons this gaming hall was so successful was because of the staff's discretion. No one used their real name here. If people had the cash and could keep their mouth shut, they were welcome. They, in turn, protected your anonymity.

He tried a charming smile. "I don't suppose there's anything I can do to change your mind?"

"I'm afraid not, Mr. Scott."

Trick sighed and inclined his head. He thanked his host and went in search of his mystery girl.

All was not lost. Only the most elite players received credit at Chao's. And judging from the ass-whooping he'd just received, this girl was elite with a capital E. Which begged the question—how had he gone this long without meeting her?

Trick knew every underground card room worth visiting on the East Coast. The dealers in Atlantic City knew him by name. He was also known by reputation at a fair number of Indian casinos, too. Without conceit, he was considered one of the best poker players in the world. That rare circle was a small community. Anyone capable of beating him should have been on his radar long ago.

And yet, here he was. He'd been blindsided tonight, in more ways than one.

Trick ordered a glass of Moutai from the bar, sipping and wondering where his mystery woman learned her craft. Some might attribute her win to luck, but Trick had played cards at a professional level for years. He knew skill when he saw it. Not that luck hadn't played a part. But even though she'd been the victor, Trick was inclined to think it had been on both their sides tonight.

Where was she?

Even his sister Maggie didn't take that long in the bathroom. He scanned the room, spotting her in the back. His mystery woman was headed in the direction of the count room.

Not good. Chao and the others didn't appreciate it when his patrons tried to go back there. Trick rose from his barstool, intending to go over and nudge her in another direction. Preferably to the Caislean, the hotel he owned with his siblings, for a late steak dinner and drinks.

She was gone. Trick blinked. One minute she was there, and the next she disappeared when two German businessmen blocked his path.

"Did you see a beautiful girl in a blue dress?" he asked one of the guards blocking the corridor to the count room. He gestured to a point past his shoulders. "She has long brown hair, blue eyes."

"Over there," the man said, gesturing to a little-used side staircase. It was the one used to bring dim sum and other hot dishes from the restaurant downstairs. And the only exit down that way led into a back alley, one even he would hesitate to walk alone.

She probably doesn't know. His mind went to Maggie, his sister. He wouldn't want her walking down that way on her own. Trick quickened his steps, hurrying down the stairs.

The kitchen was in the process of shutting down for the night. He nodded at two of the line cooks before making a beeline for the back door. A busboy came in just as he reached it.

The kid nodded and smiled, getting out of his way. Trick shot past him only to hear the distinctive sound of a chain-link fence rattling. He was outside in the alley in a fenced-in box that protected the dumpster. She was on the other side, her luscious lips parting as he skidded to a stop on the wet pavement.

The door between them was padlocked. Had the busboy let her out? *Crap.*

"So…how about dinner?" he asked from the other side of the fence, as if no time had passed.

The girl shook her head in disbelief, a smile playing on her lips. "You don't give up, do you?"

"Never been known to before." Trick grinned, drinking in her eyes. "My name is Patrick by the way."

"Hi, Patrick." She tried not to smile and failed. He grinned at her like an idiot.

Trick knew plenty of beautiful women. Models, socialites, actresses…Over the years, many of them had graced his bed, but those were lighthearted and no fuss affairs, at least on his part. His feelings had never been deeply engaged. Staring into this girl's light blue eyes, he knew she could be different.

"Why do you want to go out with me?" she asked, suspicion clouding her expression.

He laughed. "Aside from the obvious, I don't think anyone's kicked my ass so hard at cards since I was in high school."

Her head drew back. "So you're a glutton for punishment?"

"Something like that. What do you say? The cook at the Caislean makes an amazing tenderloin filet."

She was thinking about it. He could tell. "It's after midnight. The kitchen will be long closed by now."

"They'll open it for me," he assured her, deciding not to mention he was one of the hotel owners.

C'mon. Let the gods smile on him one more time.

A distant noise made her turn around. Her face shuttered, all expression wiping clean, as she stared down the mouth of the alley. He couldn't say why, but he sensed something had changed.

"Sorry." She glanced back at him almost apologetically.

Trick frowned. "At least let me walk you home or call you a car. It's not safe out here at this hour. Hell, it's not safe at noon."

"I'll be fine," she said, starting to walk away before pausing. "By the way, what is the obvious reason?"

"For me wanting to buy you dinner?" He'd wondered if she'd ask. "That would be the fact you might be the most beautiful woman I've ever seen."

Her chin dipped down briefly. She might have blushed, but it was hard to tell under the yellow glare of the streetlight.

"Well...maybe next time." She hesitated a second before rushing to the chain-link fence. Trick grabbed the links on his side as she stood on her tiptoes to reach his mouth.

Her lips were warm and soft, but the sweet pressure was too brief. She backed away, leaving him aching and frustrated.

Impulsively, he tried to grab her coat through the fence but couldn't hold on. She slipped away and was halfway down the alley before he could blink.

"You could at least tell me your name," he called.

For a long moment, the only sound was the tap of her high heels, walking away.

Halfway down the block, she turned. "It's Maria."

Then she hurried away, disappearing around the corner.

CHAPTER 2

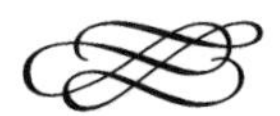

Trick summoned a lackluster smile for Solomon, the Caislean's weekend doorman. He went inside, only half-paying attention to his surroundings.

I should have climbed the fence. There had been barbs at the top of it to keep vermin out, but he should have done it anyway. He was kicking himself for going back out through the kitchen. By the time he exited the front door and made it back to the alley, Maria was long gone.

But all wasn't lost. Trick had connections in the gambling world. Sure, he'd never used them for something like this before, but his curiosity was piqued. He was going to find that girl.

The night manager waved from the front desk. Trick nodded back, doing a cursory sweep of the luxuriously appointed lobby. Normally, he'd join the front desk crew for a status update. He liked knowing how close to capacity they were each night, and whether the staff had run into any problems. This was their flagship property—the first hotel he and his siblings opened. No matter how many others they added to their prominent hotel chain, the Boston Caislean was their baby, the gold standard against which all others were measured.

But his heart wasn't in it tonight. The only thing he wanted was a hot shower and bed. Maybe a drink.

Better make it a double, he thought, starting involuntarily as he caught sight of the person who'd entered the doors after him. *I'm starting to hallucinate.* Tonight's events had clearly scrambled his brain because if he didn't know better, he'd say the girl scurrying across the lobby was Maria.

It *was* her. They were only a few blocks from the card room. She must have come this way after running an errand. There was an extra little bodega bag along with her tiny purse.

The night security guard, Juan, waylaid her before she made it halfway across the marble floor. She was only a few feet away, facing the main doors as if contemplating making a break for it. He hurried over to the pair.

"I'm sorry, unless you're a guest of the hotel, you can't cross through here once the hotel bars and restaurants are closed," Juan was saying. "Pedestrians have to walk around the building."

"Oh, I…" Maria's eyes widened as she saw Trick beaming over the security guard's shoulder.

"Did you change your mind about dinner or are you here for a rematch?"

Her mouth opened, but she didn't say anything. He enjoyed the shock on her face a little too much. *Christ, she's beautiful.*

Juan coughed, his lips twitching. "A friend of yours, sir?"

Trick nodded, excusing the man with a signal of his hand. Juan gave him a knowing glance and melted into the background, leaving them alone in the middle of the Italian marble floor.

"I take it by your expression you're surprised to see me?"

"Uh…" Maria peeked at Juan, who was chatting with the night manager now. "I am. I was just taking a shortcut. I didn't realize it was against the rules."

He folded his hands behind his back. "That's not a problem as long as you're with me."

Her blush deepened. "I guess they know you here."

"They do." He waved at the penthouse elevator. "I don't expect you to come up to my suite or anything, but we could have a nightcap on the roof garden…"

Movement near the door caught his eye. A pair of men started to enter the lobby. They must have realized it was the wrong hotel because they turned around before the doorman could open the wide, brass-lined doors for them.

When he turned back, Maria was standing close to him. She grabbed his hand. "Take me to your suite."

Trick cocked his head at her. "What?"

She gripped his hand. "I said take me to your room. *Now*."

"O-kay…" That was quite a change of heart. He pointed to the manager's hallway.

"It's this way," he said, surprised to find his heartbeat quickening.

Taking one last glance at the doors, she followed him to the private elevator that led to the penthouse floor. The door closed shut behind them, and Maria took a shaky breath.

"Are you okay?" he asked.

Her long brown hair swung back and forth as she nodded too vigorously. "I'm great."

Wondering why she was lying, Trick pressed his thumb to the fingerprint scanner.

He never got the chance to ask. She was gone before dawn.

CHAPTER 3

Tahlia needed to stop longing for things she couldn't have.

She knew better—really, she did. But resisting Patrick's charm tonight had been beyond her abilities. Being with him felt so natural and intoxicating. She'd wanted to be close to him. *Very* close.

He'd wanted her, too. He hadn't bothered to hide his fascination with her. The way his eyes would track her and the hunger in them that made her shiver.

Why didn't I stay?

She wanted to kick herself. They could be having breakfast in that massive suite right now, maybe more.

Patrick had been full of plans. He'd scheduled their entire week...dinner, dancing. It sounded like so much fun. At one point, he'd even offered to fly her to Monaco to see a *'real'* casino. She almost ran to get her never-been-used passport then and there.

But the fantasy of running away with him melted away with the dawn. As soon as he dropped off to sleep, she slipped out of bed, heading home all alone.

Tahlia couldn't put a stranger at risk that way. Especially not someone so appealing and engaging.

God, listen to me. Tahlia met the man less than twelve hours ago, and she was already acting like a lovesick schoolgirl. But like all the men she'd been interested in, this one was also off limits—for now. Things might change later. She'd lived in Boston for years, and it had been months since she'd heard from her family. Maybe they were finally backing off?

Except for that pair who'd chased her into the hotel. What about them?

Tahlia shook the idea off. *I'm too paranoid.* Most likely they were random strangers headed in the same direction as her. She suspected everyone.

Wincing, she climbed the three floors of her Cambridge walk-up replaying the night's events. She hated the sky-high heels she was wearing, but places like Chao's had expectations.

Maybe I could call the hotel and ask for Patrick? No, that was stupid. Fancy hotels like the Caislean protected their VIP's anonymity. And Patrick was clearly that. His clothes and manners —not to mention the thumbprint access to his penthouse suite—all screamed wealth and prestige.

The deadbolt should have been a clue. Tahlia always double-locked her apartment door. Opening it required two full revolutions, but this time, the door unfastened after one. Unfortunately, that detail didn't register until after she kicked off her heels in the middle of the living room.

"Time to go home, Tahlia."

Starting violently, she spun around, clutching her purse to her chest.

Her cousins were standing just past the doorway of her tiny bedroom, far enough out of sight to ensure she didn't notice them right away.

They were wearing black and grey, just like the pair following her earlier.

Her heart thrummed loudly in her ears. "What the hell are you doing here? How did you get in here?"

Cain peeled himself off the doorframe, making a production of pivoting to examine her apartment and furnishings with disdain. His brother Dante crossed his arms and stayed where he was. He always let Cain do the talking.

Cain wrinkled his nose as if he smelled something bad. "We came to take you home."

"I am home." Out of the corner of her eye, Tahlia began looking around for a weapon.

"C'mon, Tahlia," Dante said. "This place is a shithole."

Her temper flared. "*It is not.*"

Her furniture was utilitarian and no frills, but she hadn't picked it off the street. *I got it at Ikea!* That may have been bargain basement to her cousins, but it was perfectly respectable in the real world.

"It is compared to what's waiting for you," Cain said. "Come, your father wants you home. Pack your things."

She shook her head. "I don't believe you."

If her father truly wanted her home, then he would have called. He knew she wouldn't disobey him. He also knew the last way to gain her cooperation would be to send these two to fetch her.

Cain tsked, tilting his head to sneer at her. "Poor little cousin. Still clueless after all this time."

Striking with a lightning-fast move, he reached out to grab her again, but Tahlia was ready. She drew out her handheld Taser from her purse, fingers on the button trigger. It caught in the smooth fabric of his shirt, but the voltage went through the folds easily.

Contorting and jerking wildly, Cain fell to the floor.

Dante shouted, an incoherent roar, leaping over his brother. He rammed into her like a football player making a tackle, but she bounced off him, falling backward onto the couch.

Tahlia gasped, the wind knocked out of her as Dante fell on the floor after catching his foot on the throw rug.

Heart racing, she raised the stun gun for a second discharge, but he yanked it from her grasp.

"You've always been such a little bitch." Dante sneered, finally speaking. "I told Dad we should have done this a long time ago."

With a swipe of his massive paw, he slapped her across the face. Then he hit her again, his fist closed this time.

The right side of her face exploded with pain. She fell sideways with a cry, holding her hand to her cheek and eye. It felt as if her eyeball was going to fall out of her skull—the skin around it was starting to swell shut.

Blindly, Tahlia stretched her hand out, reaching under the couch cushions.

The kitchen knife she'd hidden in her sofa was one of many stashed all around the apartment. The man at the thrift store believed she was opening her own restaurant. She let him think that. It had been easier.

Dante didn't see it coming. When he yanked her shoulder, she clutched the knife against her chest.

Tahlia stopped thinking. All she could hear was her own heartbeat as she lunged, driving the thin blade into Dante's leg. Her hand lost its grip, her own momentum driving it over the handle.

There was a burning sting as the knife slashed her hand open.

Swearing viciously, Dante batted her away. The knife pulled out of the wound as she was driven back. Blood flew all over the floor and her clothes.

Dante swore. "You know, I almost felt bad about what was going to happen to you, damn bitch." He spat on her as he reached into his pocket.

He held up a syringe filled with a yellow-tinted liquid.

"No!" She scrambled away, half-crawling, half-dragging herself to the door. Her fingers were on the doorknob when he caught her, pulling her by the hair with a vicious jerk.

Tahlia shrieked, twisting and squirming to break free. The needle bit into her neck, flooding her with a cold darkness that seeped into her veins, sapping her strength.

The last thing she saw was the scratched wooden floor as it flew up to meet her face.

TAHLIA KNEW where she was before she opened her eyes. The smell and the way the cloth coverlet felt under her hands were too familiar to mistake.

I'm home.

Wincing, she sat up. The Spartan lines of her childhood bedroom came into focus.

Everything was the same. The plain furnishings and scant decor hadn't been touched. The only thing she had in abundance was books. They lined the shelves and littered the tables.

The volumes hadn't been bought for her. There was no Sweet Valley High or Babysitter's Club in the bunch. Most of them were at least fifty years old. She'd pilfered them all from their library, up until her father caught on and made her stop. He didn't like how the gaps on the shelves appeared. But he hadn't made her put these, her very favorites, back.

Her clothes were different. Her blue dress was gone, replaced by a pristine white one. There was even a pair of white slip-on shoes set on the floor by the bed to match.

Tahlia shuddered, wondering who undressed her. She hoped it was a maid, but the unceremonious way she'd been brought here meant all the maids and lower-level staff had been dismissed for the day. That was what her father always did when he hosted a special 'family event'.

Her stomach roiled as she tried to stand, but her legs could barely support her. Aching all over, she shoved her feet into the shoes and pulled herself up with the aid of the bedpost.

What the hell was in that syringe? She wrapped her arms around her middle, trembling from head to toe. The remains of whatever drug had been pumped into her were making themselves felt.

Why was she here alone? Dante and Cain dragged her all the way from Boston only to dump her in a room without a guard. They hadn't even bothered to tie her up.

Maybe the drug was supposed to last longer?

Tahlia wobbled to the door unsteadily. Whoever put her in bed hadn't even bothered to close it. Voices sounded somewhere in the distance, but she couldn't make out what was being said.

Unlike the other bedrooms in the house, hers was on the ground floor. She paused at the threshold, listening.

"It's too late!"

Sucking in a sharp breath, Tahlia shrank back. That was her uncle Lucas.

The impulse to run and hide was overpowering. *Calm down.* She needed to speak to her father. There must be a reason he'd allowed Dante and Cain to kidnap her from school.

She squeezed her eyes shut and counted to three, willing her feet to move forward. The numbness started wearing off, sending pins and needles shooting up her soles. People were moving around, but she got lucky. No one ran out to tackle her.

Inching her way down the hall, she peeked through door after door. The only visible person was outside, a fast-moving figure dressed in a suit passing one of the windows. It could have been any of her male relatives or one of the estate's many bodyguards.

The figure passed out of sight, and she unfroze. *Get moving.*

She had a tentative plan. There was always cash stashed in the drawers of her father's desk. Her purse was long gone, along with her identification, but she'd regroup in Boston. Getting back there was imperative. There was money stashed there, and another fake ID.

Like her bedroom, the door to her father's office was open a crack. He must have been out because it was usually kept it closed.

She hurried inside, running behind the desk, hastily pulling drawers open. It wasn't until after she found the money that she glanced up. The beige and green patterned Persian rug was soaked red with blood.

Her father's sightless eyes stared straight at her.

The ringing in her head was back. It drowned out all other sound. Even the bright sunlight in the room felt like it was pulling back, leaving her in the dark.

"Get that room fucking cleaned up now!"

Tahlia jumped, her head whipping to the door. That was Lucas again. He was closer now.

Go.

She bolted for the window, shoving the open sash wide. Her feet hit the ground with a little thump. Praying no one was close enough to hear, Tahlia turned and ran for the distant glitter of the private beach, the adrenaline fueling her flight.

She didn't look back.

CHAPTER 4

SIX MONTHS LATER

Trick dodged Liam's fist and pivoted on his feet, somehow managing to keep his balance while hopping a few feet away. He was back to back with his brother, as planned. Blood pumping in his ears, he reached out, taking hold of Liam's *gi*. He used it to get a better grip before flipping the much larger man over his shoulder.

Liam crashed to the floor with a grunt. He rolled and was back on his feet in a flash, but he couldn't dodge Trick's fist.

He hit him hard, and Liam went down again.

"What the hell, man?" Liam's heavy brows drew down as he frowned at him.

Trick relaxed his stance, backing away. "Sorry," he muttered.

His brother stood, cocking his head at him. "It's okay, but what happened to the light workout you wanted?"

"Upset I got in a shot?" he asked, circling Liam cautiously.

It wasn't all that common for Trick to get the upper hand in a match. Technically, he was faster than his brother, but not by much. With his superior body mass, Liam could use raw power to overwhelm his opponents, although he rarely used brute force indiscriminately. He was too skilled for that.

"*No.*" Liam's lips thinned. "I'm just wondering what's eating you. You've been quiet lately. And you were short with Hector yesterday when he came into the office to clean out the trash cans."

Trick sniffed. "I was not."

Liam crossed his arms. "Well, you didn't snap at the guy, but you barely looked at him. You hardly speak with any of the staff anymore, even though it's part of the job. All you do is hole up in your office, taking calls from your poker buddies. Have you even checked on the architect on the Sydney renovation yet?"

Shit. "I'll do that after the service." Trick scratched his head. His mind wasn't on his job, but he'd believed he'd been covering better than this.

His brother didn't move. "Is that what's bothering you?"

Trick leaned back in his chair. "What?"

"The memorial service for Maia's friend," Liam said. "I know it's sad. But we didn't know the girl. Did you even meet her before she went missing? Was she here with Maia or Peyton?"

Maia MacLachlan was the wife of Liam's oldest friend Calen. Her friend Tahlia, another graduate student at Harvard, had gone missing months ago. Today some of Tahlia's friends and colleagues were gathering at their hotel at Calen's behest. Though there was still an open investigation into Tahlia's disappearance, Calen thought having a service would help his wife with deal with her loss. Maia, on the other hand, thought getting Tahlia's friends together might spark something in their memories that would help find her.

"No. I never met Tahlia," he said, a guilty flush creeping up his neck. How could he tell his brother he was upset over someone he'd encountered *once* months ago? Especially today.

"We better hit the showers," he said, changing the subject. "The service starts in less than an hour. Peyton will have our hide if we're late."

His brother grimaced. "Yeah, she already read me the riot act about the decorations earlier. Said it was too funereal."

Trick couldn't blame Peyton and Maia for their reaction to the arrangements. It must have been difficult for them to accept that their friend was gone, especially since a body had never been found.

He and Liam parted, each heading back to their own suites to shower and dress. They met back up twenty minutes later in the hall outside the hotel's smallest salon, the one that was usually used for conferences and small reunions.

This afternoon, it was decorated in muted tones, a few tasteful sprays of flowers along the walls. The somber display was affecting. Trick fiddled with his tie, checking each group for familiar faces.

Peyton, his sister's best friend and a member of their IT team, walked over from a cluster of people near the freesia. *She is spot on.* It did look like a funeral.

"You're late," she hissed.

"Sorry," he mumbled, tugging at his collar.

"Let me," she said, reaching up to adjust it with her typical efficiency.

She narrowed her eyes at Liam as she worked, but his brother didn't even glance at her. Liam's eyes were fixed on his phone. It was rude, but Trick knew he wasn't really working. His brother hated funerals more than he did—ever since their own parents died when they were kids.

But Peyton knew his brother as well as he did. Liam would work straight through the entire event if he wasn't stopped. She took his phone out of his hand, silencing his growl of protest with a single warning finger.

"You'll get this back after, at the reception. Maia will speak first, then Tahlia's advisor from the Math Department has a few words."

She started to leave but hesitated. "By the way, Maia is fit to be tied about the invitations. If you value your life, *don't* call this a memorial or imply in any way that her friend won't be coming back."

"But I thought it *was* a memorial." Liam frowned. "It's not good for Maia to keep holding out hope. Her friend is…well, she's gone."

Peyton rounded on him, getting in his face. She reached up and pulled his forelock with a hard jerk. "Don't you dare get on your soapbox on this one," she snapped. "You do *not* know what's best for Maia. Neither does her damn fool of a husband, not this time. I agree with Maia and Maggie. It is way too soon for this. The investigation isn't closed. Ethan just confirmed that."

Liam's face darkened. "Of course Agent Thomas isn't going to tell you the truth. You're too close to this. But he's not investigating anymore. He's out of leads."

A bright red flush crept up Peyton's face. She opened her mouth, but Trick forestalled her.

"We better take a seat. I think I see Maia about to start," he interrupted.

Peyton rarely argued with Liam, but when she did—*hoo boy*. Everybody needed to run for cover. Stopping the argument before it started was the best way to go.

"*Fine*." Peyton thrust something into his hand, a card of some sort. She gave one to Liam, too—only far less gently—before walking away.

He could practically see the snarky comeback bubbling up to his brother's lips. Liam started after Peyton, but Trick snagged him by the back of his wool coat.

He gave his brother a discreet punch in his backside. "Peyton was friends with the missing girl, too," he said. "Stop being an insensitive jerk."

Liam's face softened, his shoulders dropping. "I know. I just want them to deal with it instead of keeping hope alive. It's not good for either of them to keep going on this way. Calen agrees with me."

"Well, I'm not sure I do. How long has she been missing? Less than a year?"

"You know that doesn't matter," Liam muttered under his breath. "The poor thing was probably gone after the first night. The best we can hope for now is to find the body."

Trick sighed. "I guess, but it may be too soon to make Maia do this."

Liam trudged toward the chairs. "Well, take that up with Calen. This is his rodeo."

Calen, an entrepreneur and club owner, was financing Maia's desperate search for her friend. But he himself hadn't held out much hope the girl would be found alive.

Trick didn't know all the details. He'd been outside the investigation's inner circle—Maia, Calen, and the FBI agents, his brother-in-law Jason and Jason's partner at the bureau Ethan Thomas. What little Trick did know made him side with Calen, but it still seemed harsh to say so aloud.

"I still think it's premature," he repeated before nodding at Jason and Ethan as they took the seats in front of them.

He tucked the card Peyton handed him into his pocket without looking at it.

Maia rose from the front row of seats, walking a few short steps to the small raised dais in the front of the room. Her eyes were red and she was very pale, but her voice was steady when she greeted everyone.

"I want to repeat what I told you when I invited you," Maia continued after the formalities had been observed. "This is *not* a memorial," she said with a pointed glance at her husband in the front row. "This is a gathering to remember an absent friend, one we all hope to see again someday..."

Trick's eye wandered to the right. He didn't hear anything after that. He was too busy staring at the big, blown-up color image of the beautiful brunette on an easel next to her.

"Oh my God, it's her."

All this time, Maia had been going crazy over her missing friend, and he'd been feeling guilty for not helping more. He'd been too busy searching for his mystery girl.

They were the same person the whole time.

His mind raced over the details he'd heard about Tahlia's disappearance—the blood in the living room and signs of a violent struggle.

Fuck. He was going to be sick.

Trick reached out to steady himself on the back of Ethan's chair. Even though he was seated, he felt as if the ground had given way underneath him. A tremor ran through him, and he put a hand to his stomach in an effort to hold himself together.

Oh God. All this time and he hadn't realized. If only he'd paid closer attention or even asked to see the missing girl's picture. Hell, he hadn't even helped put up fliers. Instead, he and Liam paid a few of the hotel's busboys to do it for them.

A rough hand shook his shoulder. "What the hell does that mean?" Ethan Thomas snapped.

He blinked at the agent. When Maia sounded the alarm about her missing friend, both he and Jason were drafted to help find her.

"What?" Trick whispered.

"You just said *it's her.*" Ethan held up the little memorial card where another picture of the missing girl was printed.

Trick shook off his hand, patting his pockets. He snatched his own copy of the postcard up, staring avidly at the woman pictured.

How could I have missed this?

There she was in full color. Her silver-blue eyes stared up at him above a list of personal details—her name, age, height, and weight.

Tahlia. Her real name was Tahlia. Maria was her middle name.

Is...not was. They hadn't found a body.

He took a shaky breath. Along with the physical description were the details of where she was last seen…leaving a restaurant after having dinner with Maia. The date listed was a few days before he met her.

"I saw her at Chao's after this," he said, meeting Ethan's dark eyes as he held up the card.

Which meant Maia wasn't the last person to see her before she disappeared. He was.

CHAPTER 5

Trick tried to focus on all the question's Ethan was asking, but his mind was still reeling.

His mystery woman was Maia's friend Tahlia...and everyone else in this room thought she was dead.

After seeing the amount of blood in the crime-scene photos, it was hard to believe otherwise.

"Where did you meet her?" Ethan asked, sounding more impatient than usual.

Trick blinked at him, half-suspecting it wasn't the first time the FBI agent had asked him that question.

He swallowed. His throat felt thick and swollen as if he were coming down with something. He coughed to clear it. "It was at an underground gambling hall called Chao's."

"*What?*" His brother glared at him from the couch. "You told me you only played in legal places now."

Liam and Calen had ushered him and the agents up to his office, so they could speak in private. They told the ladies he wasn't feeling well. The excuse wasn't a complete lie. His stomach was queasy at the thought of what Tahlia must have gone through in that apartment.

Trick ignored his brother. His small peccadillo was nothing considering this information.

"I'm going to find whoever did this to her," he told Ethan in a hoarse voice.

Ethan and Jason glanced at each other. "Just how well did you know her?"

"I only met her that one night...but she made an impression." A corner of his mouth turned up as he replayed that last hand in his head.

"How?" Jason asked. "Was she there with someone? A boyfriend maybe?"

Trick shook his head. "She was alone. We played each other. And she wiped the floor with me."

"Are you serious?" Ethan leaned back. "She beat *you* at poker?"

"It would be more accurate to say she crushed me." He cut a straight line in the air with his hand. "Completely leveled."

"*Wow.*" The agent was surprised, but Ethan was a pretty crap card player. Playing him wasn't much of a challenge. And it wasn't as if Trick never lost. Losing occasionally was strategic. Tahlia hadn't won every hand she'd played that night either—only the ones against him. *All* the ones against him.

"Did you say anything to her?"

"Huh?" Trick stared at Ethan.

"You didn't get mad and say anything rude to her after you lost?"

Liam scowled at the agent, but he wasn't offended. Ethan was genuinely curious to find out if he was a sore loser, because he'd only ever seen him win.

Trick laughed. "Actually, I asked her to marry me. I think I was serious, too."

He half-expected Ethan would smile or join in his laughter, but the FBI agent's expression was one of pity.

That, more than words, told him what Ethan thought of Tahlia's chances.

He held the crime-scene photo. "Is there any chance she's still alive?"

Ethan and Jason glanced at each other. They had one of those silent conversations he and Liam sometimes had when they were in the conference room negotiating a deal.

"One of you spit it out," Liam growled.

Jason cleared his throat. He glanced at Calen. "There's something we haven't told you all. The blood found in Tahlia's apartment is not all hers. Some is, we think, but a fair number of the swabs came back as male."

"Was it the attacker's blood? Why didn't we hear about this before?" he asked.

Calen held up a hand. "Jason and Ethan needed to keep some details back while they investigated, but I asked them not to share this. I didn't want Maia to hear about it."

"But if it's not all Tahlia's blood, then there's still a chance she's alive, isn't there?"

Calen rubbed his face. "Not necessarily. All the evidence proves is she defended herself. But I don't want you or Maia getting your hopes up. Only a limited number of samples were taken. By the time Ethan and Jason took over the case, the scene was cleaned up. So there's no real way of telling how much was hers."

Fuck. "So what now?"

"We're still investigating," Jason assured him.

Trick read between the lines. The 'as a homicide' was implied.

Ethan clapped him on the back. "The good news is, now we have another avenue to explore. Tahlia was a gambler. We should start combing the underground rooms and legit casinos."

Um... "I'm already on that. I've checked everywhere," he added. "She hasn't been seen since that night."

Liam swore and rubbed his face hard with his hands. The general atmosphere in the room dampened.

"I can't believe you were the last one to see her," Jason said after a long minute.

"Maybe he wasn't," Ethan mused. "What if she went back to the casino later? Or some other similar place?"

Trick shrugged. "I don't think so. I checked all the local haunts for news of her." He debated telling them about Tahlia spending the night, but he hesitated.

Only the agents need to know. It wasn't as if anyone here would judge, but those kinds of details had a way of leaking out. And as much as he wanted to think the best of people, most were judgmental. If they knew Tahlia came up to his room the night they met, they might think less of her. He wanted to protect her reputation.

"Are you sure?" Ethan asked. "Would this Chao tell you that straight out? I think we should question him and lay out the facts. He might know something."

"It's not likely, but maybe there's some detail that might help. However, Chao's not going to talk to you," Trick warned. "And he's definitely not going to let the FBI question any of his staff. I, on the other hand, am a known quantity."

Liam's face darkened. "What are you planning?" he asked.

His gaze swept over the assembled men, coming to rest on the FBI agents. "Let's just say you have your resources, and I have mine."

CHAPTER 6

Tahlia limped behind the dumpster near tears. If the bouncer saw her crying, he wouldn't let her into the card room and she *needed* to get in.

In the six months since her cousins kidnapped her, she'd lived off the grid—the cash she'd taken from her father's desk had given her a start. But it was gone now.

The first thing she'd done after escaping her family estate was to buy a train ticket to California. On her way, she made sure to pass in front of several public spaces with visible security cams. Then she'd bought new clothes and doubled back, buying a bus ticket north.

Her plan had been to wipe out her Boston bank account the next day. The minute she'd arrived, Tahlia cleaned herself up and rushed over to her bank. She'd been waiting when the manager opened the doors, but it was already too late.

Her accounts were compromised. She didn't know if Uncle Lucas froze them or if he'd simply reported her to the police.

And I came so close. The manager had been about to hand over a cashier's check for the balance of her accounts when he'd seen something on his screen. He'd hesitated and excused himself.

Her paranoia that morning had served her well. She'd snuck out of the office and into the bathroom only to see the man send in two uniformed guards after her. Somehow, she'd managed to sneak out and back to the bus station without being arrested.

She'd spent that first day sitting in an isolated corner of a random coffee shop. Later that evening, she broke into her office in the Math department on the Harvard campus.

Hidden in the back of her bottom drawer was a few hundred dollars. There was also a terrible fake ID, the first she'd bought to go to an Indian casino.

Tahlia never wanted her family to know about her gambling, so she began covering her tracks early on. The Kansas driver's license would never pass muster under scrutiny, but it was good enough to get her a hotel room.

That was her first mistake. Hotels were expensive. Staying at places with familiar names in a town like Boston wiped out a substantial chunk of her cash reserve. Terrified of losing the rest, she rented a locker at the bus station to keep it safe along with a few personal items she'd left in her desk.

She'd been too afraid of going back to her apartment for anything else. Instead, she headed to a woman's shelter.

Though jarring, things hadn't been that terrible at the shelter. The dedicated staff tried to help her. They'd offered counseling, which she turned down, as well as help getting work, which she hadn't.

Over the past few months, she'd done a series of odd jobs to supplement her meager resources. Working as catering staff was the best of these—at the end of the night, they let them take home leftovers. Not spending money on food had been a huge help, but her luck hadn't held.

One night after a long night working, the shelter had been too crowded when she'd tried to come in.

Sleeping on the streets was terrifying at first. But Tahlia coped. When it happened the second time, she'd been prepared. Eventually, she made a few friends in a similar position. Crashing in pairs was a lot safer, and she learned tricks to make it bearable.

Hiding her sex had been the key. She hadn't cut her hair but hid it, along with concealing her feminine figure in baggy men's clothing. The alternative had been to act crazy and smear herself in garbage to make herself less of a target for assault, but that wasn't foolproof. Neither was befriending a man to watch out for her. She hadn't wanted to trade her body for safety out there.

Fortunately, none of the latter options had been necessary. Her disguises worked, and she'd been able to transition from the shelter to the street and back again. Her flexibility enabled her to weather the worst of her situation.

Tahlia had debated going to her friends for help, but she'd been afraid to reach out to them. Like all her familiar haunts, Tahlia knew they were being watched. Her family had tentacles everywhere. They would never stop looking for her.

Why had Uncle Lucas killed her father? The brothers hadn't been close, but they had been allies all her life. She didn't understand what prompted that terrible murder.

There is one thing Lucas and Dad didn't see eye to eye on—me.

Giving herself a little shake, Tahlia wiped her tears, abruptly remembering where she was and what she had to do.

Desperate, Tahlia decided to try Chao's tonight. She had several thousand saved in their 'bank'. The bulk of it was her winnings from playing Patrick.

She'd avoided the gambling den out of fear that her family had learned about her illicit hobby. The purse she had been holding the night of her kidnapping contained her marker from Chao's. True, they might not recognize it for what it was, but for months she debated on whether the casino was compromised or not.

Forced to try Chao's now, she prayed the wound she'd inflicted on Dante had been bad enough to distract them from picking up her purse when they'd snatched her.

If they knew about Chao's, she lost her last best hope. But she no longer had a choice. Her funds were at critical levels. Getting ready for the night at the casino made it even worse.

Thrift shops were more expensive than she realized. It took her the better part of a day to find a black dress that fit in the bargain bins. Shoes were even more difficult. After the fourth thrift store, she settled for a pair of awful stilettos she could barely walk in.

Those shoes were her downfall. The bouncer at the door was new. He hadn't recognized her. When the heel on her four-dollar pumps broke on the steps, he turned her away.

Chao's had standards, and she didn't look like a VIP member anymore.

It's true what people say—desperation is a perfume. People could smell it on you.

Tahlia shuddered, the last traces of her crying jag wearing off. She bent to take off the broken heel.

Without tools, there was no salvaging it—not in a way that would last for more than a few steps.

Tahlia grimaced, trying to snap the remaining heel off, but unlike its partner, this one held fast.

Damn it. Huffing, she began to hammer the shoe against the concrete wall next to the dumpster.

The seventh blow knocked the thin spike off the shoe. Once she was done, she had a very uncomfortable pair of flats—but to her eye, they appeared even. She was presentable.

You can do this. Tahlia fisted her hands, giving herself a stern pep talk before rounding the corner to try again. That bouncer wasn't going to stop her this time. If he did, she would demand to see Chao personally.

She walked up to the staircase, her shoes scraping the pavement instead of tapping the way heels did. The quieter shoes saved her life. She was almost there when she realized her cousin Dante was less than ten feet away.

Tahlia reared back, diving around the corner. *Shit.* Had he seen her?

Cowering behind the dumpster, she waited for the sounds of pursuit, but nothing came.

Tahlia put her hand over her heart. They found the marker… but how did Dante know she would be there tonight? Or was one of them staking out the place every night?

The latter seemed more likely. It wasn't as if either of her cousins had jobs—not unless being an asshole counted as a profession.

Oh, my God. If her heel hadn't broken, she'd be inside now. It would have all been over.

What am I going to do now? Tahlia dug her nails into her palm, a trick she learned in childhood to jolt her brain into action. It worked.

You're going to stop being an idiot. Chao's was an institution, but it wasn't the only underground gambling den in the world. Rooms like this opened and closed all the time. The other ones she knew in Boston were defunct, but one of her online poker forums kept a running tab. Most were listed in New York.

I should have gone there from the start. Staying in Boston had been stupid. In fear and apprehension of the unknown, she'd clung to the familiar sights of her adopted city, the only one she'd ever been to outside of her hometown in Florida.

New York was intimidating to the average person, but for someone like her—with little to no experience of the outside world—it was a terrifying prospect. But Tahlia was at rock bottom. Any more bad luck and she'd be on the streets selling her body.

Wouldn't that be the ultimate irony? After years spent under lock and key, she was contemplating prostitution as a viable option.

At least I won't have to hitchhike to New York. The bus that ran from Chinatown to the city was cheap enough for her meager funds. She'd find a shelter and then the nearest underground game. Once she replenished her cash, she'd think about getting farther away—someplace warmer. Maybe Oregon. She liked trees. Or Mexico. Warm beaches had a lot of appeal to a native Floridian. Tahlia didn't look it, but she was half-Cuban and knew a little Spanish. She would get by.

Just knowing Dante was inside Chao's was enough to make her pick up her pace and get moving. It was almost as if her cousin could see her.

Enough. Tahlia was done living in fear. Her cousin survived their first confrontation, but if they met up again, someone would die. Tahlia strongly preferred that person be Dante or Cain, but if worse came to worst, she would escape again...permanently.

She wouldn't let them take her alive.

CHAPTER 7

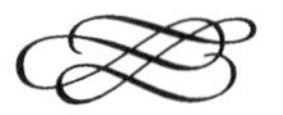

Trick was having a hard time concentrating on the plans in front of him. His eyes were blurring, and the fine letters were jumping around, but he couldn't put this off again. He'd promised Liam these blueprints would be approved yesterday.

If only the tiny text on them wasn't so small. *I have to ask those architects to send over a blown-up version.*

"Are you even listening to me?"

He lifted his head, staring blankly at his brother. When had Liam come into his office? And why was he wearing one of his charcoal Friday suits on a Wednesday?

"I'm sorry what?" he asked.

Liam clucked his tongue at him. "I've been talking *at* you for five minutes. I can't even say talking *with* you because all you've done since I walked into the room was grunt. Have you heard a single word I've said?"

"Err…"

Liam sighed heavily. "I was just telling you I looked those over yesterday and sent the approval in myself. It was the only way to keep the Sydney expansion on schedule."

"Oh shit, I'm sorry." Trick pushed the papers away. His chest tightened, the way it always did when he let one of his siblings down.

His mind couldn't focus on work. "I got a little behind," he said, dropping his pen on the desk. "I didn't get a lot of sleep last night. Won't happen again."

Liam twitched his slacks up and sat down. "Patrick, this isn't healthy."

Uh-oh. His brother had done the pant thing *and* used his full name.

"Don't take this the wrong way, but I'm not feeling up to a lecture right now."

Liam scowled. "Well, that's too bad cause you're getting one anyway...I know you were at Chao's all last night. And when you were in Miami last week, you hit every casino in town—all the illegal ones."

He sighed. "I'm a grown man, Liam. I can go to a casino if I want. It's not like I lost any money."

"I know you didn't lose money. I almost wish you had. But you didn't play at all. You were searching for Tahlia, and you and I both know she's dea—gone."

He shook his head. "Even you can't say it. And until you can, I'm not going to believe it."

Liam's eyes filled with sympathy, but he was too stubborn an ass to let it go. "You can't go on like this, Trick. I hate being painted as the bad guy because I'm realistic. Peyton is hardly speaking to me as it is. She won't even let me near Maia—as if I would ever say or do anything to hurt Calen's wife. But you two can't keep this up. Even that ass Ethan agrees with me. You need to get on with your life."

Liam leaned back, rubbing his face with one hand. "Don't get me wrong. I feel bad about what happened to Tahlia. If I could get my hands on the people who hurt her, I would strangle them with my bare hands, if only for Maia's sake. That being said, I can understand her need to keep the investigation open. Tahlia was a good friend of hers. But you only met the girl once. *Once* and look at you." He waved his hand over him. "You're a huge mess."

Trick glanced down at himself. His suit was rumpled, and he desperately needed a shave. His tongue also felt like it had a film of nasty mold over it. "So I'll take a shower. It's not a big deal. I just…"

Pursing his lip, he struggled to find the words. It was difficult with his mind so muddled. "Have you ever felt an instant connection with someone? Not like finding them attractive, although I *did* want Tahlia from the start."

He broke off and rubbed his face. "I'm not sure how to explain this. It was…as if I'd been permanently distracted, always thinking about the future. My mind was always on what was *next* and not on what was in front of me. And then Tahlia was there, kicking my ass at cards. For the first time in forever, I felt…awake. I was totally in the present with her. Does that make any sense?"

Liam didn't say anything.

Trick exhaled. "I know I sound like a crazy person."

"No, I get what you mean."

"Really? You've felt that?"

"All the time."

Trick let his disbelief show on his face. "With who?"

He hoped Liam didn't mean Caroline, the woman he'd been seeing on and off for the last year and a half.

"Never mind who." Liam glanced at his watch, waving his question away. "Should I tell Calen you're not going to make it tonight?"

"Tonight? What's on tonight?"

This time, Liam openly scowled. "It's the opening of *Eolande*, Calen's new restaurant at the Caislean New York. He flew in that celebrity chef Kari Jones to cook tonight—the one who won that television contest. Everyone is coming. Even Maia, although she hasn't been feeling well."

He wrinkled his nose. "I thought that was on Friday."

"Trick, it *is* Friday." Liam snorted. He ran a rough hand through his hair. "Maybe you shouldn't go. I swear Calen would thank me for locking you in your room tonight—every time Maia sees you, she gets worked up all over again. Ever since you told everyone about Tahlia's gambling, she's been running around trying to find out more, just like you. That's not good in her condition."

Her what? Trick frowned. "Did I miss something? Is she pregnant again?"

Liam lifted one shoulder. "They haven't said anything yet, but she's been sick a lot and she stopped drinking coffee and wine, so I'm pretty sure she's expecting."

Damn, his brother noticed everything. Trick had attended all the brunches and dinners with the McLachlan family Liam had, but he hadn't picked up on those details. And his sister Maggie hadn't mentioned anything either.

Well, Liam notices almost everything. His brother's single blind spot was how Peyton felt about him. Given the way things were going, Trick counted that as a blessing.

Liam pushed away from the couch, standing up. "No matter what, don't mention you went back to that underground casino again or Maia will want to go with you next time."

Not good. Calen would kill him if that happened. "I'll be fine tonight," he said, getting to his feet. "I'm going to take a quick nap first."

"All right. Copter leaves at six sharp. Don't be late."

He nodded, but Liam stood to follow him out to the corridor.

"And for all our sakes, please shower. The helicopter is a tight space."

"Asshole," Trick muttered, too tired to flip his brother off, before surreptitiously smelling his armpit.

Okay, Liam had a point.

CHAPTER 8

The opening of *Eolande* was splashier than he'd expected. As soon as he and his siblings approached the side door that led to the restaurant, paparazzi popped out of the woodwork to snap their pictures. Fortunately for him, his brother-in-law Jason was there. One flash of his FBI badge and the leeches scattered like rats.

Dinner was also delicious. Kari Jones, the chef, had a reputation for being a bit of a diva, but she cooked a damn fine duck breast. The hand-pulled pasta side dish was the perfect accompaniment. It was almost good enough to pull him out of his funk—almost.

All of his friends were there. Sergei and his wife were chatting with Peyton and his siblings. Calen and Maia had left their little girl with the nanny for the night. Even Gio was in town for the occasion, although his fiancée hadn't been able to leave her work to join him.

The more the wine and liquor flowed, the more the levity grew. Even Maia smiled once or twice, although his brother had been right about her not drinking. *As usual.*

Maybe he should consider giving up his search. It didn't mean he had to close himself off from the investigation. He'd keep his feelers out at all the casinos and card rooms, and he'd double the number of private detectives hired to work the case.

Whatever else was true, Trick couldn't keep burning the candle at both ends. He would just have to leave the physical searching to someone else from now on.

When everyone was kissing each other goodbye, he wandered outside the hotel's side entrance. There were still plenty of people out, but this time no paparazzi rushed him for a picture.

Enjoying the moment of solitude, he inhaled, trying to cleanse his head.

Sergei and Eva exited with Gio, chattering about the evening and the great meal.

"*Buona notte,* my friend," Gio said, coming over to administer a big bear hug. "Get some rest. You look tired," he added, before joining the others in the waiting limo.

"I will," Trick called after him. He didn't blame Gio for being in a hurry to catch his flight back to England. His smoking hot fiancée Sophia was waiting for him there.

He waved goodbye to the car as it pulled away with a wistful sigh. All his favorite people were pairing up. *And I'm still alone because someone took my maybe-soulmate away.*

If Liam could hear him now, he'd smack him, and rightfully so. Trick knew thinking that was insane. He'd only spent one night in Tahlia's company…but it didn't seem to matter.

How was Maia holding it together? He'd only been aware of this hole inside him for a few months. She'd been living with it for the better part of a year.

Maudlin now, he leaned back to study the night sky, wondering where his favorite constellations were. They were never visible in the city…

He was about to turn to go back inside when someone bumped into him, hitting his left side with a soft crash.

Trick spun, ready to apologize, when he found himself staring into a pair of wide silver-blue eyes.

"Tahlia?"

It was her—the same brown hair and big almond-shaped eyes, but she was wearing a threadbare denim jacket that was much too light for the weather.

Shock lined her too-thin face. For a moment, they simply stared at each other.

"No," she said, turning away quickly. She hurried down the sidewalk.

Trick blinked. *Holy shit*. Was he hallucinating?

"No, wait, please!" He went after her, sidestepping around a pedestrian who'd walked between them.

She was getting away. Already she was halfway down the block. Trick started to run, dodging tourists and late-night partiers when Tahlia suddenly veered right, cutting across the street.

"Tahlia!" He turned at the sound of small feet pounding the pavement behind him. Maia had spotted her as well and was running after them.

The rest of his party had finally exited the hotel. Jason was alert, his hand on his weapon. Calen was trying to follow Maia, but the crowd on the busy Manhattan sidewalk had thickened and he couldn't reach her.

"I've got this," he yelled back to Maia, waving her back.

He sprinted in Tahlia's direction. Her brown hair was visible, but she was far up the block on the other side of the street now, almost out of sight.

Male shouting and loud honking forced him to turn back around. Maia had ignored him. She followed them into the road, making a taxi swerve into the next lane—but the car that followed it wasn't slowing down.

Trick pivoted, darting back to snatch Maia out of the path of the oncoming vehicle.

Everyone was shouting. Calen ran into the street after them. Wordlessly, Trick thrust Maia back at her husband before weaving through the traffic to cross the street and run down the block.

He rounded the corner, expecting to see Tahlia, but she was nowhere in sight. He'd lost her again.

CHAPTER 9

Trick continued to search for Tahlia like a maniac, but he was soon forced to accept he wasn't going to find her. The crowd was too dense and easy to get lost in. And she *had* run away from him—fast.

When he returned to the Caislean NY, the area in front of the side entrance was empty. The doorman directed him inside, up to the family suite.

His brother-in-law Jason opened the door. "What the hell, man? Why did you take off like that? I thought you were going to get flattened by a truck."

He shrugged. "I went after her. Didn't you see her?"

Jason blinked at him. "You mean you saw Tahlia, too?"

"I knew it!" Maia was pointing at him triumphantly from the circle of Calen's arm. She twisted to punch him in the arm. "I told you it was her."

Liam and Maggie stepped into the foyer from the bar area. Their expressions were carefully blank, but Calen didn't bother to disguise his feelings.

"I don't care if it was the fucking Queen of England, you do not run into the middle of the street like a crazy woman!" he snapped. "And no, I'm not going to apologize for yelling earlier. You scared me half to death running in front of that car. If you'd been hit, two lives would've been lost."

Silence. Trick glanced at his brother, who gave him a gloating I-told-you-so smirk.

Maia rolled her eyes and smacked him in the chest before yawning. "You know we're not supposed to tell people yet. And that taxi stopped like an entire foot away from me."

"But only about two inches from Trick," Calen said from behind gritted teeth. "Because of you, he might have been hit." He turned to Trick with a belligerent air.

"It's not like it was really Tahlia, was it?" he asked, almost shouting.

Trick froze as all eyes turned to him. "Actually, I think it was. And I did run out there on my own in the first place. Sorry about that," he said, the last directed more at his brother and sister than their friend.

Calen's mouth parted. "What?"

Clearly, he hadn't been expecting that answer.

Jason narrowed his eyes. "Are you sure, Trick? You've hardly slept, and there's a lot of tall brunettes out there. Hell, there are two in this room," he said, gesturing to Maggie and Peyton.

"I'm pretty sure," he said, trying not to wince. He'd taken a nap, but for a moment, he'd doubted his own eyes.

"And she looked scared, didn't she?" Maia interjected. She took hold of his shirtfront beseechingly. The dark circles under her eyes mirrored his own. "Did you see anyone chasing her?"

A corner of his mouth turned up, but it wasn't a smile. "Just me. It seemed to startle her when I used her real name. As far as she's concerned, I'm not supposed to know it, remember?"

He put his hand on Maia's slight shoulders. "But this is good news. She's alive and in one piece...You look as tired as I feel, and no wonder with a baby on the way. Why don't you let Calen take you to your room and get some sleep while I talk to Jason and Ethan? We'll get a search plan going. By the time you wake up, we'll have it ready."

"No, I want to stay," Maia protested, but she couldn't stifle another yawn. The early stages of pregnancy zapped her strength the first time around, too.

Trick squeezed her hand, determination filling his chest. "Now that we know for sure Tahlia is alive, I promise we will find her. You can trust me on this one—I'm not going to let her go without a fight this time. But tonight, you can get some rest. We'll go over our plan with you in the morning."

"That's a great idea," Calen said, slapping him on the back before extracting Maia from his embrace. "You're ready to pass out, babe. Let's just go upstairs and I'll run you a nice room-temperature bath."

"Room temperature?" Peyton wrinkled her nose.

"You're not supposed to have hot baths when pregnant," Calen said, wrapping Maia's coat around her shoulders.

"I don't think she's going to freeze on the way to your room. It's just down the hall," Liam pointed out.

"Shut up," Calen said, flipping him off as he took advantage of his wife's exhaustion to usher her out.

Fortunately for him, Jason coaxed Maggie and Peyton into following soon after. But Trick was too buzzed with excitement and concern to do the same.

"Was it her?" Liam asked. "You can tell the truth now."

He rolled his eyes. "I'm not fucking lying, and I'm not imagining things. It was Tahlia. She's lost weight, but it was her. I would never forget those eyes. And she recognized me, too."

His brother continued to glower skeptically, but Jason wiped his chin and started to pace. "Okay, so what do we know? What was she wearing? Did you see anything that might identify her?"

Trick scratched his head. "The only thing I registered was her jacket. It was blue denim, and it didn't seem heavy enough for this weather." He closed his eyes, trying to picture every detail. "She was wearing a black skirt, and there was a blue backpack under her shoulder. That's all I remember."

Jason nodded, taking notes, but Liam was still frowning.

"So if it was Tahlia, I have a question. Why did she run away?"

CHAPTER 10

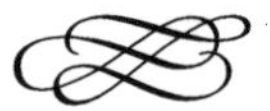

Tahlia gasped as she lowered herself into the corner cot of the dank basement room. The stitch in her side faded on the short train ride to Spanish Harlem, but her mad dash nearly wrecked her.

I am not in shape anymore. Always being hungry killed the will to exercise.

Tonight, she was lucky enough to have a room at a local women's shelter there. That hadn't been the case of late. Beds were in short supply at most of the shelters now that winter was here, but the woman at the catering company she'd been temping for made a call on her behalf. Gina wanted Tahlia to return to the Caislean in downtown Manhattan tomorrow for another event, so helping had been in her best interest.

Waitressing that wedding was supposed to be the highlight of Tahlia's week. With her earnings, she was finally going to have enough money for the buy-in at the Hammer room, the cheapest underground casino she'd found on her poker forum.

But how could she go back to the Caislean now?

Tahlia hadn't believed she'd ever see Patrick again. At least not while she was awake.

She huffed an unwilling laugh, blinking back tears. Late at night when everything was quiet, she let herself think about him. In her imagination, the night they met ended very differently.

Tahlia had spun some serious fantasies about that man, but more than anything, she'd wished for a chance to go back and explain everything to Maia, her only close friend from school.

How in the world did those two know each other?

She almost collapsed from heart failure when she ran smack into Patrick. He'd used her real name, which was terrifying after months of living anonymously.

She assumed the worst—that somehow her uncle had gotten to him, that he'd been bought off. Afraid he was about to grab her, she'd bolted. Tahlia was halfway across the street when Maia started yelling.

Her impulse was to turn back, but the sports car that nearly clipped her forced her to move. When she was safely on the other side of the road, she'd seen Patrick go back and push Maia out of the street. Maia's husband was there, too, as well as a few others who appeared familiar.

Unsure what to do, she ran for the nearest subway station.

She racked her brain, trying to remember all the people she met through Maia after her friend had gotten married. There had been a lot of new faces and names, but she didn't think Maia had ever mentioned a Patrick. And they hadn't met in person. Tahlia would have remembered him.

Maia was married to Calen McLachlan, the insanely rich son of an Irish mobster. Tahlia googled him to make sure he wasn't involved in anything illegal before the wedding. As far as the public and police were concerned, Calen was a successful entrepreneur and investor, nothing more.

His questionable reputation had been a comfort, although Tahlia hadn't thought about it that way at the time.

Her family had left her alone for a few years after she'd started grad school. Things changed in her third year. Dante and Cain started spending time in Boston. She'd gone from an average boring student to a paranoid freak who constantly looked over her own shoulder.

But right when her life started to go south, Maia met and married her millionaire. Overnight, she acquired a pack of new friends, rich and connected people who could protect her.

Perhaps that was why Tahlia continued to socialize with her long after things became uncomfortable with her relatives.

Her family's intrusive surveillance was obvious to others by then. In Tahlia's last year of grad school, her cousins and their lackeys dogged her everywhere she went. The exception had been when she'd gone to see Maia at her then-fiancé's penthouse apartment.

Her relatives also left her alone when the two had gone out for the occasional meal, mainly because her friend was always accompanied by bodyguards, courtesy of her overprotective husband.

And she's still well-guarded. Tahlia wrapped the thin denim jacket closer to her body. Maybe she could reach out now that Maia knew she was alive.

Don't even think about it, she ordered herself sternly. It was far too dangerous for all concerned.

But the weak part of her mind couldn't help picturing asking Maia for help.

Her friend would give it without reservation. That she knew already. But the image of her father's body flashed in her mind.

No. It was impossible. Going to Maia had never been an option. In fact, Tahlia clung to that friendship far too long—a futile attempt to hang on to some semblance of normalcy in a world that was spinning out of control.

I didn't even love my father. That hadn't been an easy thing to admit, even to herself. Santino certainly hadn't loved her. He hadn't even let her call him Papa or Father while he lived. Theirs had been a rigid and very formal relationship.

Her mess of a childhood was why she was a badly socialized, self-taught math geek, one who faked being normal. And then something happened. Maia had been talking to her about her new friend Eva, the wife of her husband's friend. It had been an incredible story about how a poker game saved Eva's life.

Tahlia had always been good at card games, but it was that story that prodded her to do something with her skill.

She started playing online, but the popular website she tried showed signs of being biased against the player. The odds, which she could calculate in her mind in seconds, hadn't played out the way they should have.

Tahlia decided she needed a game where she could see a person's reaction. One fateful afternoon, she took the bus to the local Indian casino. At first, she'd floundered like anyone out of her depth. But once the novelty and anxiety faded, she'd found an unexpected advantage in her sorry childhood. The way she'd grown up forced her to become an expert at reading human expressions while masking her own. It was a talent she honed at the awkward family gatherings. That ability combined with her math skills and excellent memory, and Tahlia was instantly an elite player.

That was how she ended up at Chao's playing against Patrick—because of the story Maia had told her. Somehow, she'd come full circle.

I can't go back to the Caislean, can I? Not if she wanted to avoid putting her only friend in danger. Patrick, too, apparently.

She had to stop thinking about him. As far as he was concerned, she was a ghost. A resurrection was not in the cards. Not for her.

Tahlia huddled in the narrow twin bed later that night, mentally counting her cash. She had a little over two hundred dollars left to her name. It wasn't enough for the buy-in at the Hammer room, but with luck, it might be enough to get her to California.

Flying standby on a budget airline had been her plan, but now that she'd been recognized, perhaps a bus ticket was the way to go.

But she would be much better off if she could get paid for tonight's work...

Then at least she'd have enough cash to get a room for the first night. She just needed to convince Gina to give it to her while simultaneously failing to keep her word to do a second night of work.

"No, absolutely not." Gina was adamant. The matronly redhead blew her frizzy hair out of her face, giving Tahlia a dismissive once-over before sidestepping a busboy in the busy industrial kitchen.

"You don't get rewarded for letting me down and leaving me in the lurch. Two waiters and a line cook already called in sick."

"I am so sorry." The guilt was eating her alive, but she needed that cash.

Gina put her hands on her hips. "I can still use you."

She waved at Tahlia's nondescript dark pants and top. "You could even wear that. At this point, I don't care."

Tahlia winced and glanced around at the other waitstaff, but none of them were paying them any attention. Everyone was scrambling to get ready.

She twisted her hands together. "I hate this. I've never broken my word before. I always keep my commitments, but I need to leave town and the money would be a huge help."

Tahlia followed Gina around the counter where the chef was preparing line after line of puff pastries. He was garnishing them with thin slices of foie gras and a berry compote.

Her stomach rumbled. Tahlia tore her eyes away from the food. "It's not like I'm asking for a handout, or even an advance. I only want last night's pay."

Gina stopped. Her expression was not precisely sympathetic, but she didn't appear ready to shell out any cash either. "See here, I hire from that shelter you've been staying in a lot. I get that a girl just has to disappear sometimes. I want to help, because believe it or not, I've been there. But I need to balance that with keeping a roof over my kid's heads. Besides, I don't have any cash on me. And there's no way in hell I can drop everything to go get it now."

She broke off to gesture to the chair near the back door. "The way I see it, you have two choices. You can go sit in the corner and wait until this is all over, or you can borrow a white shirt from my bag and grab a tray. If you do the latter, at the end of the night, I'll give you the full two days wages, plus a small bonus you better not mention to any of these other guys. So what do you say?"

Tahlia took a shaky breath, surreptitiously glancing left and right. It felt as if there was a bright spotlight on her, but she knew it was all in her head. What if Patrick or Maia showed up as guests?

"I'll do it, but if I suddenly dive under a table, please pretend not to notice."

Gina nodded, patting her on the arm. "Thanks. These two weddings are huge for us. It's the first time we've worked this hotel. If we can get on the Caislean's list of preferred vendors, we'll be all set—I can pay the kid's college tuition without my deadbeat ex-husband's help. Now go to it."

Tahlia nodded, tying the apron around her waist.

A few hours later, Gina kept her word. Tahlia had her wages plus an extra thirty dollars. It had been an extremely stressful evening, but she was reasonably certain no one spotted her. Feeling hopeful for the first time in memory, she went to the bus station where she'd stored the bag with the rest of her cash.

Her plan was to leave immediately, but the next bus heading to California didn't depart until the following morning.

Staring forlornly at the closed ticket counter, she debated going back to the shelter, but it was after one AM. The doors closed at midnight.

Resigned to spending the night on a wooden bench, Tahlia found an empty seat in a relatively well-lit corner of the station.

This is fine. She'd slept in much worse places. Before Gina vouched for her at the last shelter, that list included the sidewalk in Williamsburg and a cardboard box behind a dumpster in Dumbo. This would be a cakewalk compared that.

Slipping her arms through the straps, Tahlia hugged the bag to her chest before settling down for the night, vowing not to sleep. But the long hours on her feet took their toll. She drifted off despite the bright light behind her lids.

A slight jostling woke her a few hours later. Tahlia opened her eyes with a start, but it was too late. A knife was cutting the second strap of her backpack. Before she could react, it was pulled away from her.

"No!"

She shot to her feet, pounding after the scumbag stealing all her worldly possessions. Yelling incoherently, she reached out, the tips of her fingers grazing the back of the dirty black hoodie he was wearing.

Before she could get ahold of it, she felt a hard shove from behind. Tahlia went down, landing on her knees. An intense stabbing pain arced up her left leg as it struck the flagstone.

Red flashed across her vision as she parted her lips in a silent scream. Gasping and sobbing, she tumbled forward, hitting the floor hip first. She couldn't prevent her head from following it. It struck with force on the stone tiles.

For a moment, she lay there, too overwhelmed to move. Tears streamed down her face, obscuring her vision as a second man ran past.

All she registered was a flash of silver piercings in a gaunt acne-ridden face. He gaped at her before following the first assailant.

The pair disappeared before she could pick herself up.

CHAPTER 11

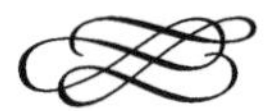

Trick was multitasking like a freak. He'd just finished a conference call with the contractor on the Sydney expansion while drafting a pleading message to the great Chao himself.

He hadn't wanted to go back to Boston. Tahlia was in New York and as long as she was, it was where he needed to be. But he couldn't run the investigation alone and his most trusted contacts in law enforcement, his brother-in-law Jason and his partner Ethan, were based in Boston.

Missing persons was not their purview, but he and a few of their high-powered friends pulled a few strings to get them officially assigned to Tahlia's case. After he and Maia saw Tahlia in New York, they'd spent most of their after-work hours on it as well.

Right now, the two FBI agents were camped out on the couch and pair of love seats that formed the conversation nook in his office. They were poring over evidence photos and making calls, but after his latest move contacting Chao, he was regretting suggesting they make this their home base.

The call he was desperately waiting for came a few minutes later.

"We have an agreement," Chao said in Mandarin.

He rose from his leather office chair, turning his back to the agents to face the floor-to-ceiling window. The Boston skyline was growing steadily darker as the last fingers of sunlight dipped below the horizon.

"Thank you," he said in his terrible Mandarin accent. "I'm very grateful. I'll forward the details later tonight."

He released a pent-up breath before hanging up with exaggerated casualness. His act didn't fool them. The agents hadn't missed the exchange. They were both staring at him.

"What is it?" he asked, sitting back down, shuffling the pile of papers on his desk as if searching for something.

Jason tsked. "Nice try. Spill."

He scratched his head. "How did you know something was up?"

"We're detectives," Ethan said flatly.

"Not good enough. Seriously, what gave me away? I wasn't even speaking English or Russian or any of the other languages you know," he said, gesturing at Ethan, the resident linguistics expert.

Ethan's fine dark eyebrows rose. "It's not what you said, it's how you said it."

Damn. They were good. *Or I'm terrible.* Clearly, his poker face didn't extend to phone conversations. Either way, Trick couldn't keep the truth from them now. He just hoped they wouldn't arrest him for what he had planned.

"Fine. You remember when we were brainstorming that night I ran into Tahlia? How I decided to check in with all my underground gaming contacts in New York?"

"I do," Ethan said, leaning back on the love seat and crossing his arms. "I also remember you promising to share whatever you heard from them."

"If any of that info had panned out, I would have. But then I had another idea..."

Jason narrowed his eyes. "I know that look. What are you up to?"

Trick leaned back in the chair and stared at the ceiling. "I decided to set up my own underground casino."

"Patrick..." Jason rolled his eyes. "You know that's illegal. If I let you do something like that, your brother *and* your sister would have my guts for garters."

"Not if I didn't plan on keeping the money," he said, holding up a finger. "For official purposes, it's listed as a charity event."

"You already set it up?" Ethan was shaking his head.

Trick loved these two, but he couldn't let these two by-the-book law officers derail his plans.

"It goes down next week. I found a little place in Chinatown, and I've been blasting it on all the poker forums I belong to and then some. I'm spinning it as a ladies' night special. Any woman who comes in the door gets a hundred in complimentary chips."

"Only a hundred?" Ethan scoffed.

"I thought a thousand would be too suspicious."

"A hundred may not be enough. Go with a grand. So what was the call in Chinese about?" Jason said, shuffling some papers.

"I asked Chao for a favor."

"Oh, I do not like the sound of that," Ethan said.

"Yeah, no kidding," Jason agreed.

"No matter what you do, don't tell Liam," Trick said.

"You didn't sign away your shares of the Caislean, did you?" Jason asked.

"Of course not," he tsked. "But Chao's daughter is getting married, and she loves the Caislean ballroom. The waiting list is booked up for the next five years."

"Oh, is that all?" Jason appeared relieved, but Trick wasn't finished yet.

"Well, technically, the date she wanted wasn't available, but as it happened, the people who booked it are over a month late with the final payment. I'm going to bump them to the medium blue ballroom and refund them the difference."

Trick had a great poker face, but his brother-in-law knew him too well by now. "What's the catch?"

He grinned. "The people who booked it represent a prominent conservative congressman. He wanted to celebrate his thirtieth wedding anniversary with a big bash."

"Liam is going to kill you." Ethan's grin was downright gleeful as he leaned back on the cushions. "I'll let you borrow my gun if you want to defend yourself. Aim for the big bit."

Trick snorted. On his brother, that was pretty much everywhere. "Maggie will back me up on this one. The congressman only wanted the big to-do because he was caught having an affair with a college-aged staffer last year. He'll just have to make do with the smaller ballroom."

Jason adopted the same amused posture as his partner. "Ethan is right. You're going to need the gun. So what favor is the great and powerful Chao doing for you, and is it worth it?"

"He's sending out an email."

"An email?" Jason was skeptical. "You bumped a congressman's pearl anniversary for an email?"

"His what?" Ethan asked, eyeing at his partner sideways.

Jason twirled his pen. "That's what the thirtieth wedding anniversary is called. The first is paper, the tenth is tin or aluminum, twentieth is china. You know…"

"No, I don't know." Ethan rolled his eyes. "What man under seventy knows shit like that?" He turned to Trick and mouthed *'whipped'*.

Jason threw one of the decorative silk couch cushions at him. "I know because Maggie books a lot of the major events for the hotel chain. Rich people like to crow about how long they've been married so she has to know all that stuff. It bleeds over."

Trick nodded at Ethan. "We had a third wedding anniversary celebration here last year with a budget in the six digits. The traditional gift for three years is leather. They went the S&M route for decor."

Ethan laughed, a booming sound that filled the room. "Fucking rich people," he said, subsiding. "Although come to think of it, that's a party I would want to attend."

"It was a lot less fun than it sounds," Trick said, fiddling with a paperclip. "Anyway, on very rare occasions, Chao sends out notices for elite events. Those are by invitation only. Being on the list means you're a high roller."

"And is Tahlia on it?"

"She left an email, but there's no way of knowing if it's real or if she even checks it. Not everyone leaves a real one—not if they don't know how to cover their tracks."

"And you do?"

"I refuse to answer that on the grounds I might incriminate myself. Chao finally agreed to send my notice to his list."

Jason smirked. "So long as you give him the most exclusive wedding reception venue in town for a song. How much is he paying exactly?"

Trick coughed. "Nothing."

Jason howled.

"What's wrong?" Ethan asked with a frown. "It's just a room. How much can it cost?"

Jason held up a hand. "That grand ballroom books for ten grand *minimum,* and that's just for the room. Add two or three hundred a head for the meals and booze..." He shook his head. "Liam is going to kill him."

"Wish it was the other way around," Ethan said, not quite under his breath. "Tahlia better check her damn email."

Trick gripped his pen tighter. "If she doesn't, there's still the poker forums..."

Ethan adjusted his collar and held up his phone. "Well, since you shared, I suppose I will, too. Just before your little conference, the medical examiner finally forwarded the bloodwork from Tahlia's apartment."

He frowned. "I thought you had that already."

"Only the blood types. After talking to Maia, I played a hunch. I asked them to retest for a familial match."

What the hell? "You think a relative attacked her?"

Jason flicked a glance at his partner. "One of the first things Maia told us was to take a closer look at them. She said Tahlia never talked about them, just about her mom who died when she was little and the maid who acted as nanny to her. She was tight-lipped about the rest of the clan. All Tahlia ever said about them was they lived in Florida, on an estate."

"And?" Trick was on the edge of his seat.

"Well, Maia distinctly remembers two occasions when Tahlia wanted to leave some location because she thought she saw one of them here in town."

"Just seeing one of them was enough to make her bolt?"

"Apparently. So we had retested the blood for a familial match, but there was a big backlog."

"And?" Was Ethan trying to give him an aneurysm?

"It was a match, probable first cousin."

Unbelievable. "Why am I just hearing about this now? Have you arrested him?"

The agents exchanged a glance. Ethan crossed his arms. "It's complicated."

Trick swore. "How complicated can it be?"

Why weren't they jumping up, ready to chase down the bad guy? It was what they did—what they lived for.

Jason held up a hand. "Tahlia has at least a dozen cousins. And they are loaded and lawyered up the wazoo. For fuck's sake, they have more lawyers than Calen. Plus, there's one more thing you seem to have forgotten."

Trick waited, biting the inside of his lip.

"What?"

"Based on the limited sampling, most of the blood was male, not female. If anyone is dead, it's this cousin. Which means she may have done him in."

What the hell weren't these two telling him?

"So what does that mean? Now you know she's alive, you're after her for murder?"

Jason and Ethan exchanged another loaded glance.

Fuck.

CHAPTER 12

Tahlia limped along the street, taking the back entrance to the shelter. She checked her reflection in all the storefront windows she passed. Unless someone stared closely, they couldn't tell she was injured. There was no hint of her bruises on the surface, at least not yet. Tahlia didn't know if that was a blessing or a curse.

Being beat up might help garner some sympathy with the shelter staff, but bruises wouldn't help her get work, not in catering. Servers were required to be presentable and nondescript. That was why she was going to the shelter. It was Gina's day to volunteer in the kitchen.

"Jesus H. Christ." Gina took one look at her before wrapping her in a bear hug against her expansive bosom.

The uncharacteristic show of affection crumpled what little resolve she had. Tears streaked down her cheeks as she sobbed in the older woman's arms.

"What happened? And why are you limping?"

Tahlia sniffed hard. "I fell. Or to be more precise, I was pushed. Two men mugged me and took my bag. I have nothing left now."

"Oh, sweetie, I'm sorry." Gina ushered her into the adjoining office. She sat her down on the little couch in front of the desk adorned with an ancient PC computer. "Wait here. I'm going to make you a hot coffee with extra cream and sugar."

"I take it black," Tahlia said, scrubbing at her wet cheeks.

"Not today you don't. You need the calories."

She caught Gina's sleeve. "Wait. Can I do some more work for you, please?"

Gina tsked and patted her on the head. "Not today, sweetie. You can barely walk. But don't you worry, once you stop limping, I'll be slapping a tray in your hand. Now, why don't you go ahead and do some faux online shopping? Pick out a pair of shoes and a hot dress you can't afford. That always cheers me up."

"It does?"

"Sure does, sweetie. Now go on."

Tahlia sniffed and nodded. She hobbled to the office chair, browsing as directed on the ancient computer, but stopped when Gina came back with the coffee.

"I talked to the day manager. She's out on the floor now. I'm afraid they don't have a bed for tonight, but you're in luck. You can have that couch."

Gina pointed to the worn brown sofa by the door. "I've napped on the thing myself. It's no worse than one of the cots from the main room. If you fold those long legs of yours, you'll fit okay. Plus, you can play solitaire on the guest account. Sorry, it's too old to support any other games," Gina finished with a nod at the computer.

Tahlia smiled wanly. "Thank you. And if you ever change your mind, my offer still stands to balance the account books for this place or the catering company. I'm very good at math."

"I'm sure you are, but we pay an accountant for that. Just focus on resting up."

Gina left her alone after that. Dejected and in pain, Tahlia tried to regroup. After a long nap, she drank the cold coffee Gina left on the desk and even played a few hands of solitaire, but it was dull after the thrill of poker against human opponents. Especially card sharks like Patrick…

That night playing him had been the most thrilling of her entire life. *So far,* she told herself sternly. She needed to stay positive. There would be other nights like it. This was only a temporary setback. She'd heal up and go back to work for Gina long enough to earn bus fare to California.

Once there, she'd hit a few Indian casinos. Mexico might be fun to visit but seemed too dangerous for an inexperienced traveler like her to settle in, so she'd search for a real job in Europe or Canada. Also, the only foreign language she was truly fluent in was math…

On impulse, she logged into the email account she'd created for her poker alias. Despite not using the account for anything but poker, she had a ton of spam, most of it for online gaming sites.

If only I'd saved a little credit on one of those, she thought. But now she didn't even have cash for bus fare, let alone a credit card. Not that any of her accounts were safe to use. The only ones she had were in her real name.

Deleting one particularly egregious email, she scanned the rest of the subject lines. One jumped out at her. *Ladies Night Special Event, Manhattan.* The email was from the King of Spades, the special account that belonged to Chao's casino.

She opened the message. It was addressed to her gambling pseudonym Maria Diaz.

A complimentary thousand dollars in chips to any women who enter the doors before ten pm. No minimum buy-in. Ten Grand Pot. Elite players, by invitation only.

"What the hell?" she said aloud. Who in their right mind would give away that much cash to every woman who came to play?

Skeptical, Tahlia checked her favorite poker forum. News of

the game was all over it. The free chips were dismissed as a promotional stunt. Various users claimed the list had no women or at most one or two. The no-minimum buy-in was also being picked apart. Chao's elite table in Boston had a five-hundred-dollar minimum.

Her skin began to prick with excitement. The game was local and just a few days away. The address was less than ten minutes by train. Walking it would take her less than a half hour. She wouldn't have to borrow subway fare.

She glanced down at her worn black pants and thin denim jacket, and her heart sank. This game was a godsend, but she wouldn't get past the bouncer in these clothes. Thanks to the mugging, they were the only ones she had.

When Gina came in to tell her lunch was ready, Tahlia pushed herself to stand despite the pain. "Gina, do you by chance have a dress I can borrow?"

The peal of laughter was answer enough. Tahlia quickly masked her disappointment. She was being presumptuous.

"I'm sorry. You've done so much for me already. Please, forget I said anything."

"Oh, sweetie, it's not that. You're welcome to anything in my closet, but none of it is going to fit you. All my dresses would hang on you like a tent," she said, eyeing Tahlia's svelte form. "But maybe my daughter has something that'll do. It'll be short on you, though, so I better lend you a razor, too. You need one."

It was nothing less than the truth, but for some reason, Tahlia found that hilarious.

Laughing was surprisingly painful. She'd forgotten her injuries. But she put her hands on her ribs and kept laughing anyway.

CHAPTER 13

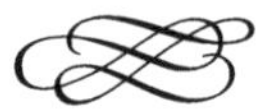

Trick squinted at the grainy video feed on Ethan's tablet. "Why didn't you let me buy new cameras?" he groaned.

How would he be able to tell if any of the women arriving was Tahlia with this crap resolution?

"The bureau doesn't have as much money as the Caislean. Especially for an off-book sting operation," Ethan replied.

The agent was busy setting up his surveillance equipment on the empty prep table. They weren't serving a formal dinner, only drinks. They had the kitchen to themselves.

"I wish you would stop calling it that," Trick groused. "You promised to give Tahlia the benefit of the doubt. It's not like you have enough evidence to charge her with anything. You don't even have a body."

Ethan's lips flattened. "You're starting to sound like Calen and Liam when they start throwing their weight around. Do me a favor and don't start acting like them now, too. You need to focus on ID'ing the girl and convincing her to trust you. Whatever she's mixed up in is bad. That lot in Florida is a nasty bunch."

Trick flicked Ethan an annoyed glance, but he nodded. He didn't need to be told there was a lot at stake.

After the blood results came in, Jason and Ethan reached out to the authorities in Florida. They wanted to know which once of Tahlia's cousins was missing, presumed dead. The bureau in Miami promised to check it out, but instead of hearing back from them, they were contacted by a prestigious Manhattan law firm.

A flood of threats followed. Jason and Ethan were strongly advised in the harshest legalese not to contact any member of Tahlia's family. Harassment of any kind would be met with a legal shitstorm of biblical proportions.

It's like they didn't care about the welfare of one of their own.

Trick had met families like that before—the kind that dealt with their own problems internally. If Tahlia was that problem, then she needed help. A lot of it.

"She was so thin and pale the last time I saw her, like she'd skipped a lot of meals." *My last meal was steak.* As if on cue his stomach began to hurt.

"Not by choice, I'm sure," Ethan observed quietly, giving him a once over before continuing to fiddle with the surveillance equipment.

He shook his head. "I don't like the idea of anyone going hungry or being out in this cold without a warm coat, but the thought of *her* in those circumstances…shit, it keeps me up at night."

Ethan sighed, coming up behind him. "You've given this girl her best shot to come in out of the cold with this setup," he said, gesturing at the feeds that covered every angle of the makeshift casino floor. "But you need to be prepared. There's a chance she may not show tonight."

Trick waved away the complications. "If she doesn't come, I'll try again in another neighborhood. Is Jason ready?"

"Yeah, he's behind the bar. I wouldn't order anything complicated if I were you. His cocktail-making skills are total crap."

"I know." Trick wrinkled his nose, remembering a sad attempt at a Rob Roy that turned his stomach. "Remind me why he's out there playing bartender instead of you?"

"Because the most elaborate thing I can do behind a bar is pouring a pint." Ethan adjusted his tie.

Trick snickered. "I hate to break it to you, but you're kind of shit at that. The last one you poured me had way too big a head."

Ethan snorted and shoved him toward the kitchen doors. "Get out there and mingle, but keep out of sight of the entrance. If your girl shows, we don't want her to make you and bolt before we can stop her."

Trick peeked through the small porthole in the door. In the short time since he'd last checked, the crowd had grown. The room was busy enough to blend into now. Without another word, he pushed open the swinging door and went out to walk the floor.

Maybe I should open a real casino. This place had once been a well-known card room, but in the last couple years, the clientele had dropped off until it was almost dead. Consequently, asking to borrow the venue had been easy. The proprietors welcomed his input, seeing it as an attempt to breathe new life into their spot. They were going to be pleased. Though his name and reputation pulled this crowd in the door, it was the little touches he'd added that kept them.

Smoking artisanal cocktails served over dry ice were being handed out by waiters in dapper twenties dress. Every blackjack table was full, and he couldn't even see the craps table behind the throng.

The baccarat group was still a little thin, but it was steadily building up. The sound of roulette table spinning underscored the droning murmur of conversation.

According to the doorman, over half a dozen women claimed

their thousand dollars in chips. One or two turned their chips over to the boyfriend or husband they had accompanied, but the rest hung onto them. Trick eagerly checked out those four, mixing and talking with all the guests he knew by name, but none of the women were Tahlia.

Too wired to relax, he wandered to the bar to ask his brother-in-law for a beer. He handed him a cognac instead.

"You need to relax," Jason leaned in to say quietly. "You're starting to sweat. If your pretty face wasn't so familiar, this crowd would be looking for an exit right now. Some of them are probably half-expecting a police raid."

Trick glanced around. One of the guys he knew from the pro-circuit was scrutinizing him and Jason closely. He smiled reflexively, lifting his glass in friendly salute before downing it. The man relaxed and turned his attention back to his game.

"Better," Jason muttered, pouring him a refill. His eyes were fixed on a point behind his right shoulder. "Now keep that up when you talk to Tahlia. And for God's sake, don't rush over there. Let her come to you."

Picking up his glass, Trick turned around, trying to project an air of careless unconcern when the reality was he was burning up to know if Jason was right. He sipped and sauntered, slowly making his way to the cashier, where a slim brunette in a black dress was standing with her back to him.

It is her. He couldn't see her face, but his heart was beating too fast for it to be anybody else. Tahlia was claiming her complimentary chips. When she turned to face him, her eyes were on the chips. They shined brightly as if she was near tears.

Tahlia was blinking rapidly, clutching the small tray as if it was a lifeline. He was in front of her before she was aware of him.

"Hello, Ace. Care for a rematch?" he asked softly.

She gasped, her silvery-blue eyes dilating as recognition

washed over her face. Reaching out reflexively, she shuddered and swayed.

Concerned, he put out a hand to steady her. The second he touched the soft skin of her upper arm, he relaxed. An odd mix of giddy contentment flowed through him. She reacted, too, sagging into him as if she needed the support of his arm.

"Why don't we sit down?" He gestured to the alcove, where a private poker table was cordoned off with a black velvet rope.

She glanced around as if assessing the room for threats, but Tahlia allowed herself to be led to the booth behind the ropes. He ignored the many pairs of eyes that followed them as they took their seats.

The crowd was avidly curious to learn who had earned a seat at the prime table. Little did they know this entire setup was all about her.

Trick waved over a waiter. He said something in a low voice, sending the man rushing off to the kitchen.

He turned back to Tahlia, taking in all the changes in her since they'd last met. She was so much thinner. Her cheeks were sunken, and there were dark circles under her eyes that hadn't been there before.

And was that a bruise on her hand?

"Is Maia okay?" she asked. "You *do* know her, right?" Tahlia's husky voice quavered.

He reached out and took her unbruised hand. Her fingers were ice cold. Chafing it with both of his, he nodded. "I do. And she's fine. She's worried about you, of course. I was, too, when I realized you were the friend she's been searching for all this time."

Tahlia's mouth opened and closed. She seemed at a loss for words. Wiping her eyes, she blinked rapidly. "I'm glad she's okay. Tell her I'm sorry for worrying her…it couldn't be helped."

"You can tell her yourself," he told her, but his words made her tense up.

"I can't," she sniffed.

He leaned in. "Yes, you can. I have friends who can help you. Some of them are here tonight. All we want to do is help."

Tahlia stared at him, a little crease between her fine brows. "Who are you?"

"I'm Patrick, remember?"

She laughed and swallowed. The amount of strain she was under must have been enormous because her world-class poker face was nowhere in sight. Her emotions were raw, right on the surface for him to see.

"Yes, but how do you know Maia?"

"Oh." He sat up. "I'm a friend of her husband Calen. He and my brother went to school together. Maia might have mentioned me by my nickname, Trick."

Those amazing eyes widened. "*Trick*, Patrick, that's you. I…uh, I've met your sister. You own a hotel, or rather a lot of hotels." She snorted lightly and coughed, seemingly embarrassed.

It confused the hell out of him. Her reaction read more like dismay.

Trick squeezed her hand again. "I am part owner of the Caislean chain, along with my brother and sister. And you are a brilliant mathematician just a few dissertation chapters shy of getting her Ph.D. from Harvard."

Her blush was instantaneous. "I'm not *Good Will Hunting*. I just like math."

Delighted with her response, he let go and motioned to the waiter, who was hovering a few feet away. The man set down a large vanilla milkshake in front Tahlia.

"Maia said they were your favorite," Trick explained with a little shrug. He nodded at the sealed deck on the table. "You can't wipe the floor with me again on an empty stomach."

"Thank you." She drew the glass closer, her full lips wrapping around the red straw.

Okay, bad idea. Trick could feel his IQ taking a nosedive.

He forced himself to open the deck of cards. When it was safe, he turned back to her, shuffling automatically. He didn't even want to blink, almost as if he were afraid she'd disappear before his eyes.

The fluted glass was almost empty before Tahlia spoke again. "That's a nice technique," she said.

"Not nearly as good as yours," he replied, adding a flourish he'd spent weeks perfecting as a teenager.

Her lip quirked. "You've never seen my shuffle."

"Well, actually, I meant your card-counting technique, but I'm willing to bet you have an impressive shuffle, too."

"As a matter a fact, I do know a few tricks, but I don't count cards."

Trick laughed aloud. "Oh, come on. Pull the other one."

"I don't—not consciously anyway. I've just always been very good at calculating odds and have a good memory. Plus, I'm lucky. That's what my Ama used to call me. She said I was her lucky penny."

Her eyes grew distant, the tiny spark of exuberance he'd glimpsed when he shuffled the cards fading away.

"Was Ama your mother?"

Tahlia jerked as if he'd interrupted her woolgathering. "No. She was our housekeeper. But I suppose she was sort of like a mother. As close to one as I had."

"And your father?"

Tahlia turned away, her eyes gravitating to the exit. "He's dead."

Like any gambler worth his salt, Trick knew he'd just played a bad hand. It was confirmed when she shot up from her seat.

"Wait," he said urgently, taking her hand.

She hesitated, whirling to face him with a disturbingly blank stare.

Trick recognized that look. Over the years, he'd seen it in the face of a lot of women, the ones who came to the hotel trying to get away from abusive husbands or boyfriends. They all wore that same expressionless mien.

He'd always attributed that unnerving blankness to too many horrors either seen or experienced. A body could only take so much before it went numb.

"I meant what I said," he said, infusing his voice with all the persuasion he could muster. "I can help. Believe it or not, I have some practice getting women out of trouble. And if you need even more backup, then my friends are ready and willing to do whatever you need."

He leaned closer and lowered his voice. "Two of them are here. They're FBI agents."

At the mention of law enforcement officers, Tahlia's mouth slackened. "Patrick, how could you?" she cried.

Crap, that was badly done. Of course she thought she was in trouble. Someone most likely died in her apartment the night she disappeared. He shifted, prepared to block her if she bolted.

"Believe me, these two are on your side. One of them is my brother-in-law. The other is his partner, and both owe me a favor. A big one."

He paused, stroking her wrist with his thumb. "I know what happened in your apartment. Someone broke in, forcing your window. The lock was broken. A second-floor apartment is more secure than one on the ground floor, but it's still accessible for a determined thief. He was waiting for you inside."

Tahlia sat frozen.

"It was one of your cousins, wasn't it? Which one?"

Her lip trembled, and she mouthed something.

"What was that?" Had she said a name?

She cleared her throat, scanning the room as if checking for eavesdroppers. "I said there were two of them waiting."

That last was a ragged little whisper.

Trick stifled the rush of adrenaline that made his blood run fast and hot. He'd never been this angry in his entire life—which was exactly the wrong reaction at this moment. The last thing he needed was to scare Tahlia off because of his lack of discipline.

It was make or break time.

"Tahlia, we don't know each other well, but you can trust me. I've only scratched the surface of the shit storm that is your family, and I know you can't face them alone. Not with their resources. But money and power I've got and let me tell you...I would bet everything I had on you."

She blinked a few times. "So you're offering to stake me?"

One corner of his mouth lifted. "That's an excellent way of looking at it. I want to pit my resources against theirs."

Tahlia hopeless expression didn't change. "Patrick, this isn't a game. There's no chance of winning here. Those people—" She broke off and shook her head. "I don't even know how to explain who they are or even *what* they are."

Trick wasn't the hotel's top salesman for nothing. "Things seem bad now, there's no denying that. And maybe I'm not enough to instill much confidence. After all, you kicked my ass the one time we played. But I'm not stupid enough to think I can take on your family on my own. In my business, I've learned you are only as good as the network of people at your back. Talk to my brother-in-law Jason and his partner Ethan. I may not be able to convince you to accept my help. They are another story."

He leaned forward, lowering his voice conspiratorially. "I'll never admit to this in their presence, but they are damn good at their jobs. The very best. Talk to them and see how you feel. You have my word that if you want to walk away afterward, I'll see to it that you have whatever you need. Cash, fake IDs—hell, you can take my damn car."

Tahlia smile was small, but her eyes flashed like diamonds. Her teeth ran over her full lower lip as she appeared to think it over.

"Is one of these FBI agents you think so highly of the bartender over there?"

He cocked his head at her. "How did you know?"

She turned, checking out Jason at work from the corner of her eye. "I don't think the lady he just gave a drink to is enjoying it judging by the face she's making. Can't really blame her since he used gin in a cosmopolitan. A real bartender wouldn't make that mistake. And you would only hire the best mixologists under normal circumstances, wouldn't you?"

He shouldn't have been surprised to learn she was incredibly observant. Poker players studied human behavior, searching for the minute tells that gave away a bluff. But noticing that a bartender across the room used the wrong liquor was above and beyond.

Now he knew he was in love. Their children would be brilliant, beautiful, *and* self-aware.

"Jason and Ethan will be on your side, as am I," he promised. "You don't have to do this alone."

This last made her stop and think. He could see the longing in her expression.

No one should have to face the kind of crap she was up against on their own.

"I don't want anyone to get hurt because of me." There was a hint of an unspoken *again* in her voice.

Okay, there was no fucking way in hell he was letting her out the door without him now. He'd pick her up and carry her to the kitchen himself if he had to.

"And I don't want you to get hurt because you were afraid of taking help I'm more than capable of giving." His eyes bored into hers, willing her to gamble on him. "I wasn't kidding before. I do have experience against crazy family members and stalker types. More than you would guess. But you don't have to take that on faith. If you don't want to talk to Jason or Ethan, I can have Maia on the phone in under a minute. She'll vouch for me."

There was a long pause as she fiddled with the napkin under the milkshake glass. "You don't need to do that...I'll talk to your friends, but I can't promise anything."

Trick was thrilled, but her expression tightened as if she immediately regretted her decision. Patrick hurried to his feet, putting his arm around her. He was eager to get her in the back before she changed her mind.

They were halfway across the room when the lights went out. A blow to his back threw him off balance.

It happened so quickly he didn't have time to brace himself. He hit the floor hard, and it knocked the wind out of him.

Using the reflexes honed by a thousand sparring bouts with Liam, Trick rolled, flipping to his feet the way he did whenever his older brother knocked him to the ground.

When he could breathe again, he called out to Tahlia, but it was doubtful anyone could hear him over the pandemonium breaking out.

People were screaming. There was the sound of running feet and glass breaking over the clatter of poker chips hitting the floor. He reached out, but the only thing his hand encountered was a man's pant leg.

"Tahlia," he called out again, hands out. He grunted when another body—a large man—barreled into him, hitting him on the shoulder. But this time, Trick kept his balance, automatically pivoting to minimize the impact. It happened so quickly he almost missed the burning sting on his palm.

Ignoring the sensation, he raced toward the faint light that shone into the room briefly when the kitchen door swung inward. Ethan was back there holding a flashlight.

"*Patrick*." Jason was calling out for him.

"I'm over here," he said, tracking his brother-in-law's voice back to the bar.

They met in front of the swinging door. "Lights! We need light. I lost hold of Tahlia."

Jason grunted. He pushed the swinging door open where Ethan was holding the flashlight up to a breaker box.

"Do you have another flashlight?" Trick asked. He needed to get back out there to find Tahlia.

The beam of light swept over him. "Why the hell are you covered in blood?" Ethan barked.

Trick glanced down at the ominous red slash staining his otherwise pristine white shirt. He swore aloud. "Fuck! My hand—I thought that hurt too much."

"What the hell happened?" Jason asked.

"Give me the flashlight. I need to get back to Tahlia," he pleaded. "Someone is running around with a knife out there."

"Hold up," Ethan snapped when he reached out to take the torch from his hands. He flipped a few switches, and light flooded the kitchen. It came on in the main room as well, where the screaming abruptly stopped.

Ethan and Jason right behind him, he burst past the swinging doors. The makeshift casino was a mess.

The guests were milling around nervously. The waiters were trying to restore order by picking up the broken glasses and strewn poker chips. Letting them take care of it, he ran back and forth across the space until he caught sight of a brunette standing near the window with her back to him.

"Tahlia!" He hurried over and took hold of her arm.

The girl turned, startled. It wasn't her. "I'm so sorry," he apologized, backing away quickly.

Jason was right behind him, shaking his head. Tahlia was gone.

TAHLIA RAN DOWN THE ALLEY, holding her aching hand against her chest. The man who'd grabbed her in the dark had twisted it so hard she was worried it was sprained.

When the lights went out, she'd been surprised, but not scared. At first, it appeared to be a random fluke. Then someone shoved her and Patrick, knocking them to the ground.

The impact stunned her. She landed on something rectangular and hard. It felt like a phone. She'd reached for it, intending to try and use it as a flashlight, but before she could press any of the buttons, the assailant reached down, capturing her arms in a painful grip.

Tahlia reacted on instinct. Instead of fighting him, she'd launched herself up, jumping into the man's arms. She crashed into his chest, her fingernails raking across his face. He was wearing night-vision goggles.

Tahlia snatched them off with her free hand, tossing them aside while simultaneously twisting in his grasp. The move surprised the man enough to let go.

Blind in the dark, she stumbled into other casino-goers, escaping serious injury through sheer dumb luck.

She ended up walking into the bathroom door next to the bar. Moving quickly, she locked herself inside before crawling out the window and down the fire escape, tossing the phone into her purse and kicking off her borrowed heels along the way.

Tahlia prayed Patrick was all right. The man who attacked them might have a gun. She had no idea.

It's okay, he'll come after you. Patrick and the others would be fine as long as she wasn't there.

Her feet were already aching from running along the hard, unforgiving pavement. Trying to find a place to hide, she ducked into the open space between two buildings only to find the way barred by a chain-link fence.

She almost turned around to backtrack, but the sound of

pursuit spurred her forward. Panting, she ran and began to scale the fence, heedless of the spikes poking out from the top.

Nimble and in decent shape from carrying loaded catering trays, Tahlia climbed without incident, but she misjudged her footing while trying to clear the top. She half-slid down the other side, scraping the spot under her breast with a spike on the way down.

Disoriented by the sudden pain, she fell the last few feet, landing on her foot awkwardly before tipping backward into a pile of garbage.

Momentarily dazed, she lay there catching her breath until the fence rattled. She jerked, her eyes flying up to meet a savage face. A dark-haired man gripped the thin steel wire. He sneered at her and began to climb.

Scrambling to her feet, Tahlia tried to run, but each step was agony. The foot she'd landed on was having a problem supporting her weight.

"No."

Tears streamed down her face. It was over. She wasn't going to get away this time.

But Tahlia didn't stop. The instinct to survive was too strong to give herself up. Not after what they had done to her father.

The anonymous brick buildings ahead of her were dark. She had no idea where she was or how to find help.

A thump sounded. The man jumped the fence, clearing the garbage she'd fallen into easily.

Please, God. After so many months successfully evading capture, it couldn't end like this.

She didn't know if anyone up there heard her or not, but her prayer was answered in the form of an open doorway on her left.

The upper stories of this building were lit. Praying she'd find an occupied office or a security guard, Tahlia shot through the door, only to find herself at the top of a dimly lit wooden staircase. The bottom disappeared into complete darkness.

There was no time to second-guess her choice with pursuit so close behind. She started running down the stairs.

"*Hey*!" the man shouted, careening after her.

Ignoring him, she jumped down.

It was a huge mistake. Tahlia landed on her bad foot. It folded underneath her. She lost her balance, coming down too hard on the next step. The brittle board under her splintered, throwing her against the rail.

The rickety structure was too weak to withstand the impact. Her body plowed through the flimsy barrier. Unable to catch herself, she sailed over the edge and to the floor below.

Tahlia's scream was cut off when her head rapped on the concrete twice, despite an effort to brace herself. Winded and racked with pain, she lay there, stunned.

Get up. Ears ringing, she tried to stand, only to collapse back down on the ground. Dizzy and unable to see, she crawled under the stairs, her entire body blazing in pain.

The last thing she heard was the pounding of feet on the stairs over her head.

He was coming.

CHAPTER 14

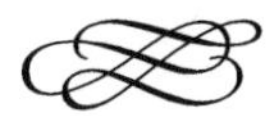

Trick rechecked every inch of the casino twice over. Tahlia was gone.

"They came for her," he repeated, pacing the kitchen. Ethan and Jason were on the phone. He didn't know who they were talking to, but whoever it was, they were too late.

Fuck. He'd had his arm around her and then boom! Someone literally snatched her from his grasp.

Ethan looked up. "The locals are setting up a search grid. We'll go building to building if we have to."

Trick shook his head. His instincts were screaming. "It won't do any good. Whoever took her was a pro. He knew enough to take out the lights with us unawares and to come prepared for the dark."

They found a pair of night-vision goggles under a stool at the bar. That more than anything sent a chill through him. He couldn't decide whether it was a fear or an icy cold rage. Either way, he refused to let it overwhelm him. Now was the time to think and plan.

I'll contact every criminal I know and make them spread the word. A million dollars for Tahlia's safe return, no questions asked. It would probably fail, but at least it was him doing something.

"Damn it," he hissed aloud, trying to come up with other ideas.

I need Liam. His brother was an overbearing ass sometimes, but he was also a mover. Liam made things happen. No one had ever been able to stop him from getting what he wanted.

Trick reached into his pocket to make the call. His phone wasn't there. He patted down his suit and swore. It must have slipped out of his pocket when he got knocked to the ground.

He stuck his head in the main room. The only people left were the waiters and dealers. The rest of the guests had left already, each one cleared by Ethan before they let them go.

"Did anyone see a phone?"

The staff shook their heads in turn, one offering to help him search.

"Hey, man," Ethan interrupted.

Trick held out his hand. "Where did you find it?"

"Find what?"

"I thought you had my phone," he said, frowning. "Can I borrow yours to call Liam?"

A flicker of distaste crossed Ethan's face. The agent and his brother still weren't getting on.

"I'm coordinating with the locals. The phone in the kitchen works. What happened to yours?"

"I don't know. It's been missing since I got tackled. For all I know, our perp picked it up." He scowled. If that was the case, then the phone was sitting in a dumpster right now.

"Or another guest took it. I can have it traced if it's still on," Ethan offered.

"Can't hurt, I guess," he said, walking to the kitchen.

Trick was still trying to reach Liam in Boston when Ethan rushed in.

"*Hey*. Your phone is stationary almost four blocks from here."

Ethan pulled on his jacket. "Jason, head's up! We're going out with the locals."

"You don't think the perp still has it, do you?" Trick refused to get excited over the possibility.

Ethan grimaced. "We won't know till we check. C'mon, get your ass in gear."

Grateful to be moving, Trick followed. A uniformed police officer was waiting outside. He was holding a pair of black high heels.

"Where did you find those?"

"Around the corner near the fire escape," the man answered.

Trick swiveled to face Ethan. "Where is that?"

"Outside the bathroom," he answered, gesturing for him to follow him.

Another officer was staring up. The ladder on the fire escape was pulled down.

"Is this the way he brought her down or did she get away on her own?"

"I don't know, but check this out." Ethan shifted a few yards down, bending to pick up a discarded poker chip. He straightened and pointed down the alley. "And your phone is that way."

The next breadcrumb on the trail, he thought, climbing into a police cruiser with Ethan.

Another car followed them. They drove a short distance before Ethan told the beat cop to stop outside the open door of a nondescript apartment building.

"Stay in the car," Ethan ordered him, gesturing to the officer to follow him.

Fuck that. Trick climbed out of the backseat with the others, a belligerent scowl on his face.

He slammed the door behind him. Ethan turned and swore. "Fine, asshole, but if you get your head blown off, I'm not going to be the one to tell your sister," he spat. "At least stay up here until we clear the building."

The doorway opened onto some sort of basement. Trick caught a glimpse of a decrepit staircase before Ethan led the officers down. They were all holding their flashlights and guns the way cops did on detective shows.

A minute or two later, a sickly fluorescent light turned on. One of the cops must have found a switch.

"Trick."

Ethan hadn't shouted loud, but Trick knew he'd found something. He bounded down the stairs, hopping over a missing step. Ethan was crouched next to the space under the stairway, surrounded by the local cops.

Trick pushed his way past them. "Tahlia!"

She was crumpled in a little ball covered in dirt with a smear of what appeared to be blood on her face and hand. Ethan was taking her pulse, but she didn't react until he shouted. She groaned.

Shit! He crouched next to Ethan. "Tahlia, are you all right?"

At the sound of his voice, she stirred and blinked up at him. For a second, her eyes cleared and she appeared to recognize him, but then her lashes fluttered closed as she slumped over unconscious.

CHAPTER 15

A whispered argument pulled Tahlia from sleep.

"I'm not leaving Calen," a woman hissed. "So you can go back to work or go bother Liam for a few hours."

Blinking, she opened her eyes to a bright sunlit room. Tahlia was in a huge bed almost bigger than the entirety of her old bedroom in Cambridge. The coverlet was a crisp pristine white, the kind she'd only seen in pictures of fine hotel rooms.

"Tahl?"

She turned her head to see a very pregnant Maia MacLachlan sitting in an armchair next to the bed. Hovering in the doorway to her right was her husband Calen. He was standing just in front of Patrick.

Patrick looked so relieved. His smile was small but filled with joy.

Tahlia burst into tears. Arms encircled her awkwardly. Maia had climbed on the bed and was trying to hug her, but the baby bump was getting in the way. For some reason, that made her cry harder.

Her whole body shook as she pressed her face against Maia's

thigh. Her friend made incoherent soothing noises, in between hisses ordering the men to leave.

Long minutes passed as she sobbed uncontrollably. It was as if a dam inside her burst. Tahlia hadn't cried when she was attacked in her apartment or at any time on the streets. It was only now she didn't have to be on guard that she allowed herself to break down.

For the moment, she was safe.

Eventually, the storm passed. Wrung out, Tahlia hiccupped, shivering in the aftermath. Sniffing, she raised her head to see how many people had witnessed her lapse in control. Thankfully, she and Maia were alone.

"I made them leave," Maia said, her sweet little elfin face as warm as Tahlia remembered.

"I'm s-sorry," Tahlia sniffed, moving her hands to cover her face. She winced at an unexpected pain. There was a brace strapped to her left wrist.

Maia rubbed her back. "It's a sprain, but it's not as bad as the one of your ankle. You also have a bandage for a deep scrape over your ribs, a few of which are bruised, but not cracked—I had cracked ribs once; it hurt like hell. You've been in and out the whole night. Our doctor took a scan of your head. You also have a mild concussion, but you're going to be okay."

If she'd been unconscious, how mild could it have been? Tahlia shifted on the bed with a grunt, pulling her bandaged wrist closer. "The man wrenched it," she mumbled.

"What man?" Trick demanded from the door.

"I told you to wait outside," Maia admonished with a scowl. She pointed at the door. "*Go*. I'll tell you when you can come back."

In the doorway, Trick compressed his lips, giving Maia a look of mingled frustration and indulgence. He nodded and retreated, pulling the door partway behind him.

"Close it for real this time," Maia said in a loud voice. There was a beat before the door snapped shut.

"Pregnancy makes you bossy," Tahlia joked weakly.

"I am enjoying the power trip," Maia said, sounding adorably smug. "But it doesn't work on Calen anymore. Not since the doctor ordered me on bedrest."

Guilt tightened her chest. "Oh Maia, you shouldn't be here. You need to rest."

Maia gestured to the California king. "Hey, I'm on a bed."

Tahlia frowned, taking in the room around her. Everything was obviously expensive but nondescript and impersonal. This wasn't her friend's penthouse.

"Um, where is this bed exactly?"

Maria patted her hand. "You, my dear, are in the inner sanctum —the penthouse floor of the Caislean in Boston."

"I'm in *Boston*?" In Patrick's hotel no less.

Well, that explained his hovering presence. Tahlia bit her lip, examining the dark mahogany furnishings and tasteful paintings on the wall.

This place screamed money and prestige. She felt as if she was soiling it just being here.

Maia gripped her hand. "I wanted you to come home with me, but Trick kicked up a fuss about having you here instead. It *is* a secure building, especially at the penthouse level. There is even on-call medical staff. That's the reason I let him win." She shrugged, stroking Tahlia's hair.

Tahlia pulled away. "I must be filthy." It was as if a grimy film was enveloping her body. Her hair was hanging in greasy clumps. Someone had wiped her face and arms with a damp cloth, but she needed a shower…followed by one or two hot baths.

"You're fine," Maia said. "But there's a nurse waiting to tend to your every need. I'm sure she can help you bathe if you want to get clean." She broke off and grinned, leaning conspiratorially closer. "At first, the agency sent a young male nurse, a rather handsome one. Trick took one look and sent the poor man away, insisting on a replacement. He said you'd be more comfortable with a female nurse—as if he would know."

"He's right." She would have felt uncomfortable having a male nurse help her bathe. No one had seen her naked before. She'd never even changed in a locker room in front of anyone because she'd been homeschooled.

Maia waved that away. "Doesn't matter. It's Trick's reaction that counts. I've never seen him act like that before. He's got it *bad*."

Blushing, Tahlia averted her eyes.

"I can't believe you met him playing poker," Maia continued. "He's an excellent player. He wins huge tournaments all the time, but you creamed him right out of the gate."

Tahlia's brow creased. "He told you about that?"

"Oh, yes. It was almost as if he were bragging about losing to you...and I had no idea you even knew how to play."

Chagrined, Tahlia pressed her lips together. "It was a secret."

One of many.

Maia nodded as if she understood. "We were pretty shocked to discover Trick was the last person to see you before you disappeared."

Her chest constricted. "He wasn't exactly."

Tears stung at her eyes again in defiance of her belief she was completely spent.

Her friend didn't say anything. She just held her hand and waited.

"They're crazy," Tahlia confessed in a whisper. Her heart raced, the panic clawing at her as if trying to stop her from saying it aloud.

"Who is?" Maia asked. "Is it your family?"

She nodded, too overcome with rolling waves of adrenaline to speak. Talking about her family always terrified her—and that was by design.

The refrain of *'family first'* had been drilled into her head since before she could walk. To her family, it wasn't just a motto—it was an all-encompassing way of life. Absolute loyalty was the rule. She was never supposed to speak about them to an outsider. Revealing their darkest secret was enough to make her spiral, even after they made their enmity toward her clear.

"You can tell me anything," Maia assured her. "And I won't share it with anyone else if you don't want me to—not even Trick, no matter how hard he pushes. You say the word, and I zip my lips and throw away the key."

That was a sweet offer, but Tahlia wasn't sure if it was a good idea. She was a wreck both physically and mentally. As much as she wanted to avoid dragging anyone into her mess, she needed time to recover and regroup. Holding back while she was near these kind people might make things worse.

"No. I want you to tell Patrick. He thinks he can help me." She broke off and stared at her hands. "That's because he's rational. I could see the gears turning in his head when we played. He's quick and takes risks, but he operates in a totally logical way. But my family doesn't respond to rational. They're flat-out insane—"

She broke off, swallowing reflexively.

Maia squeezed her arm. "It's going to be okay. We can protect you from whatever they throw at us."

She shook her head. "You don't understand. It's not one or two of them. It's *everyone.* They are all mental because—and I can't believe I'm saying this out loud—they worship the devil."

Maia blinked, her lips parted and pulled down.

"Well, not the devil," Tahlia amended. "It's a demon to be precise."

Whatever Maia had expected to hear, it hadn't been that. "As in a cult?" she asked, her nose twitching.

A shuddering sigh escaped her. "I guess that's close enough. There's no church or magnetic leaders. No one talks about it openly. It's a secret, but all the men and most of the women—they worship this particular demon. They think he really exists."

"Why?"

It was a fair question. Despite knowing what they did, the reason hadn't been discussed in her presence. It had taken her years to piece together an answer. "In exchange for their devotion, our family is supposed to prosper. Every investment succeeds, we're blessed with good health, disasters don't harm us, etcetera, etcetera. But that means they have to give the devil his due or it all goes away."

"*Huh.*" Maia frowned, seemingly at a loss for words.

"I told you it was insane." Tahlia collapsed back on the pillow. Her confession had drained her. All she could do was lie there, overwhelmed by the surreal nightmare that was her life.

"Why do they want you?"

Tahlia couldn't tell her the reason. It was just a guess on her part in any case. Any chance for real answers died with her father.

"The other members of the family couldn't believe it when my father let me go off to school. No one leaves. No one has friends outsides the family, or a life of any kind. When they grabbed me, they drugged me. I woke up in my bedroom at home in Florida. No one was there guarding me. I wasn't tied up. I just walked out into the hall and down to my father's office. I needed money, so I took it from his desk. He always had at least a grand or more in there. That's when I saw he was there."

"Your father?"

"Yes," she whispered. "On the floor, already gone. He died *horribly*. Something must have gone wrong. It must have been chaos. It's the only reason I got away."

"Oh, Tahlia." Maia's thin arms wrapped around her, squeezing tight around the safe unbruised area above her elbows.

"I think my uncle Lucas did it. I'm not sure. As far as I knew, they got on well enough, but I've been avoiding everyone since I came to school. They must have had a falling out."

She laughed hoarsely. "If Lucas had his way, I would never have been able to come to Boston to school at all. He's cold and cruel—a complete misogynist. If I'd been his, I'd have been feral. He was against letting me learn to *read*. He said I was never going to need to know how. His sons have tormented me since I was a little girl, but he is so much worse. I don't know why he wants me, but whatever the reason, it must be why my father's dead."

CHAPTER 16

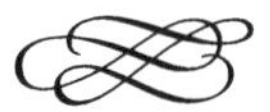

Trick felt like he was ready to crawl out of his skin. He told himself he was being crazy. The streak of madness running through him was obvious, but knowing it was there did him no good.

Tahlia was safe here in the suite adjoining his in the hotel he *owned*. That should have been enough to soothe him. But after seeing her hurt on that basement floor, he'd been spiraling with self-recrimination.

"I should have had armed guards and metal detectors," he said, still in disbelief at the brazen way the hired thug circumvented their security measures. "Then that asshole wouldn't have gotten away."

Trick was trying to save Tahlia. Instead, he'd given the assholes pursuing her the opportunity they'd been waiting for. His lack of preparation and foresight led to her getting hurt.

Calen and his brother Liam exchanged a glance. They'd been keeping vigil with him since they flew Tahlia here on the corporate helicopter.

Liam leaned against the back of the couch. "You have to stop blaming yourself. You couldn't have known they'd attack out in the open like that. Not to mention both Jason and Ethan were there, and they didn't notice anything shady and that's their *job*," he pointed out.

He clapped Trick on the shoulder. "We won't make the same mistake here. I've got the penthouse floor locked up tighter than Fort Knox."

"I know that," Trick replied, rubbing his face. "But it doesn't change the fact she's lying in that bed because of me."

"Tahlia will be fine." Calen held up his phone. "Eric is on his way back here to check on her again, but he gave her the all-clear last night. She just needs some time to recuperate."

Eric Tam, a concierge doctor who worked for the hotel sometimes, examined Tahlia while she was in and out of consciousness last night. In addition to her numerous physical injuries, he declared her malnourished and suffering from clinical exhaustion.

Trick checked the clock on his phone. "Speaking of time..."

"You agreed to let Maia have a half hour with her," Calen reminded him.

"And it's almost up," he said, staring at the closed door to the bedroom.

"Let Maia do her thing," Liam urged. "She has a much better chance of convincing her to spill the real details of what's going on than you do."

"I know that," he muttered, wondering if Calen's wife was getting anywhere.

They *were* friends, but Tahlia hadn't confided in Maia before now. According to Calen, his mystery woman had always been skittish in company. It made sense now, of course. Tahlia had been keeping a tight lid on a troubled past. She was used to deflecting any personal questions, never revealing any details about herself, let alone her true feelings.

No wonder she has such an amazing poker face.

He checked the time again. Calen tsked and shook his head. "Believe me, it's better not to push when a woman is in a vulnerable state. You don't want to overwhelm her."

Trick rolled his eyes. "Oh, for fuck's sake, that's the exact opposite of what you did when you met Maia and you know it."

"That was different."

"*How?*"

Calen wisely didn't answer.

A knock at the door signaled the arrival of room service. "Finally," he said, going to open the door.

But it wasn't Constance, the maid assigned to the penthouse floor. It was Ethan, and he appeared more grim than usual.

"What is it?"

The FBI agent nodded at everyone in the room, except Liam. "I got some of the blood work back from the basement. It's not all hers. Our perp was in there."

"*What?*" They'd assumed Tahlia managed to escape her pursuer before her accident.

"How do you know that?" Liam asked.

Ethan opened a file folder he was holding. "There was fresh blood in two places. One was under the stairs. All of that was Tahlia's."

Trick rubbed his face and reminded himself she was awake and talking in the next room.

Ethan took a picture from the file. "But there were a few drops at the very bottom of the stairs, too. They belong to this motherfucker. Meet Tommy Casey. He did a four-year stretch upstate for assault and battery, and he has a string of lesser crimes on his rap sheet. He's been keeping his nose clean the last few years, but according to rumor, it's because he graduated to the big time."

"So he's local talent?" Calen asked.

The agent nodded. "Not affiliated with your family, I assure you," he told him with a little smirk. "Whoever is after Trick's girlfriend must have hired this guy to snatch her. He almost succeeded, but Tahlia got lucky. She knocked a step loose when she fell over the rail."

"That was lucky?" Trick scoffed.

Ethan shrugged. "Tommy boy must have missed the gap in the dark. He fell down the stairs, landed at the bottom. My best guess is that he fucked himself up bad enough to abort the mission. Or else, he heard something that spooked him. Whatever the reason, he bolted without getting what he came for."

That something was Tahlia. "Where is he?" Trick growled.

Ethan shrugged. "For now, he's in the wind. We've got an APB out on him and we're running down known associates, but it could take a while. But if we do dig him up, there's a chance we can lean on him and get him to give us some dirt on his employers."

Damn. "What chance do we have of flipping a career criminal? Do you really think you can get him to testify against Tahlia's family?"

The agent shrugged. "I guess that depends on whether our hired gun thinks we're more dangerous than they are."

Trick's hand fisted involuntarily. Something told him that wasn't going to be a problem. He'd just need five minutes alone with Tommy Casey.

A door opened behind him. Maia came out of the bedroom. She closed the door behind her.

He was next to her before the door clicked shut.

Maia held up a hand. "Stop. She's already asleep."

He swore.

Maia grabbed his sleeve, turning him around to face the others. "She was wrung out after our talk. Let her rest."

Ethan shifted his weight. "Did she tell you anything that explains why her family is after her? Or is it someone else entirely?"

"Oh, it's them." She patted her stomach, screwing up her nose. "You are not going to believe this..."

CHAPTER 17

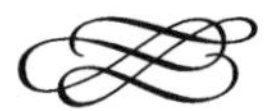

The pillow he put over the top half of his face had drifted over his mouth. Trick sat up, smacking his lips together, trying to clear his tongue of the fuzz he suspected came from accidentally licking the thing in his sleep.

He hadn't meant to drift off. He'd been waiting for Tahlia to wake up, but she'd slept long enough for him to get tired. *I was only going to close my eyes for five minutes.* Somehow, that turned into over two hours of sleep on the suite's couch according to his watch.

He glanced over the back of the sofa. *"Hi."*

Tahlia spun on her heel next to the food-service tray. She had a fistful of French fries in her good hand.

Her hair was wet and her skin possessed the freshly scrubbed look of someone who just stepped out of the shower. She was also pale, and much frailer than he remembered. The only color on her face was from a bruise high on her cheek.

"Hi." Her voice was muffled, her mouth half-crammed with cold food. She swallowed hastily.

Trick got to his feet, waving at the plate he'd ordered before her nap. "Don't eat this. I can get something fresh and hot up here in less than ten minutes."

Tahlia coughed, blinking. She reached for the pitcher of water on the cart and poured herself a drink.

"I'm sorry. I didn't mean to startle you," he said, putting his hands in his pockets before coming around the couch. "I was waiting for you to get up, and I accidentally fell asleep on your couch."

Tahlia cleared her throat, her fine features tight and uncertain. For a moment, she stared, holding her injured hand against her chest. "I'm great with this burger, thanks. This isn't your room? I mean, it resembles it, but it's laid out differently..."

A corner of his mouth lifted. "All the suites on this floor are similar. I wanted to put you in my room, but decided it was too presumptuous. "

She blushed, much-needed color returning to her cheeks.

Trick pointed to an adjoining door. "My room is through there." He cocked his head at her, gesturing for her to follow him so he could display the twin lock. "There is one of these on both sides. Both have to be undone to pass through. Yours is locked, of course. Mine will stay open in case you need something—just come on in, day or night. If I'm not there, I'm on the floor below in my office."

Normally, that wouldn't have been the case, but he was taking a break from his heavy travel schedule for the foreseeable future. Liam had agreed to take over the next series of on-sight visits to the hotels abroad, and his sister Maggie was handling their many conferences.

Tahlia's lips parted, a slightly hunted expression flicking across her face.

Trick winced. "Unless you think that's totally creepy. If you'd be more comfortable somewhere else, I can move you to another room," he added hurriedly. "We have over two hundred of them."

She shook her head. "No, it's nice of you to put me up here. I'm just a little embarrassed that everyone knows."

"That everyone knows what?"

"That I came up here with you the night we met and..."

He stepped closer, putting his hands on her shoulders. "We didn't do anything. Just talked." *And made out for a few hours before going to sleep.*

She toyed with the cotton of her sleep shirt. "I know...but no one will believe we didn't sleep together."

He walked closer, until he was close enough to touch her. Fingering an almost-dry strand of her hair, he stared down into her eyes, drinking in their startling silver-blue gleam. "I told Jason and Ethan you were here that night after the game, but no one else. I asked Juan, the security guard you met, not to mention it to anyone outside of law enforcement. Maia and Peyton have no idea. Neither do my siblings. The only reason I told Ethan was to make sure he would be able to retrace your steps that night. He's also aware that nothing happened. I made that clear."

Tahlia frowned. "Why?"

"Because I didn't think it was anyone else's business but our own. The agents will keep it to themselves—not that they're in any position to judge. Trust me on that."

"*Oh*. Um...thank you."

He sighed. Her reaction was so telling, and she didn't even know it. "You don't have to thank me for that. I know you regretted coming with me. I knew it that night, as soon as the elevator doors closed on us."

Startled, she met his eyes.

He inched closer, his hand lowering to wrap around her waist. "That's another reason I told the agents. You came with me because you felt threatened, didn't you? Even earlier in the alley, you were on edge. And in the lobby again, you kept looking over your shoulder. Maia said your family was in the habit of having you followed."

He paused, savoring the feeling of her in his arms, wishing he could crush her against him. But she was still too fragile. "I wish I'd known about them that night. If I had, I wouldn't have let myself fall asleep. And I certainly wouldn't have let you leave."

Tahlia blinked, her eyes brightening with tears. "I did want to come upstairs you. You're the one who didn't want to rush into bed. As I recall, I threw myself at you."

He moved a hand to her chin. "And you were nearly irresistible. But I slowed things down because I could feel something was off, not because I didn't want you."

He'd desired her that night, and he still wanted her now. Desire, lust, and half a dozen emotions he couldn't name were there in between them, thickening the air. He doubted it would ever go away.

But there had been a recklessness to her that night that caught him off guard. He wrestled the devil, turning down what she offered. But his instincts had told him if he slept with her, he'd never see her again. That hadn't fit with his plans.

Speaking of which. Trick took hold of her hair, twisting and wrapping the long length of it around his fist. Leaning over, he bent to kiss her, stopping when he was just a hairsbreadth away, letting her close the small distance between them.

For a second, he believed she wouldn't, but then a fairy's wing brushed him as she stood on her tiptoes to reach him.

Her lips touched his, the lightest and sweetest of pressure. That was all it took. Lust roared, drowning out his intention to handle her with care. Trick flattened his hand against the back of her head, pressing his lips down more firmly.

His tongue licked and bit, demanding entry. Tahlia obeyed, parting her full lips to let him in.

His response was completely out of proportion with the act.

One kiss should not make him feel like a conqueror, but it did. His blood ran fast and hot as he plundered, coaxing and seducing Tahlia into kissing him back.

She did, but tentatively, just like their first encounter so many months ago. Her hesitation only made him hungrier.

He'd grilled Maia on the men in Tahlia's life. As far as she knew, there hadn't been any. Perhaps there had been someone significant in Florida, but in Boston, she'd lived like a nun.

It was startling to realize how much he liked that.

Trick didn't think of himself as a chauvinist. He'd hooked up with a lot of women, and he appreciated the bold ones who knew what they wanted and weren't afraid to take it.

Nevertheless, something about Tahlia's obvious inexperience pleased him inordinately.

She's with you. It's not one-sided, he assured himself as her tongue shyly stroked his back. Though circumstances had pushed her into his arms, they did have a connection. Neither of them would deny that.

Tahlia shivered, straining against him. She put her hands against his chest, making him glance down. The wrap on her wrist reminded him to take care. He pulled back abruptly, breathing hard.

"Sorry," he apologized, taking her bandaged hand in his. "I don't want to aggravate your injuries."

Abashed, Tahlia backed away. "Now that you mention it, I could use a little more ibuprofen."

"Are you sure you don't want anything stronger?" he asked. Eric had left a bottle of codeine for her.

She shook her head. "I met one or two people on the streets who got there after getting hooked to an opiate after an injury. I don't want to tempt fate. Ibuprofen is fine."

Turning, she glanced back longingly at the unfinished plate of burger and fries.

Trick jumped into action. He got on the phone, and then quickly ordered a fresh plate over her objections. "Trust me. Our signature burger tastes a lot better fresh and hot."

She pursed her lips. "I don't want to waste anything. The kitchenette has a microwave," she pointed out, waving at the elaborate string of appliances on the far end of the counter.

"And you're welcome to use it if you're still hungry after the fresh one comes," he said, winking.

He could feel her reluctance as she picked up another cold fry from the plate. She chewed walking around the suite, her bare feet sinking into the plush carpet as she examined her new home.

The floor plan of the suite was open, with a tiled kitchen area partially separated from a sunken living area. The bedroom was separated by a pair of French doors. Unlike his room, this suite didn't have a separate office. There was a desk and reading nook in the bedroom.

The knock announcing the arrival of Tahlia's food came in record time. It was as if the kitchen had been waiting for the call—which they were. The Caislean staff was well trained, and they'd taken an avid interest in Tahlia's situation.

Preparing a memorial for a beautiful girl, only to have her come back from the dead, would make anyone curious.

He thanked Daran, the night butler, for the tray and set it on the kitchen counter by Tahlia with a flourish. "Now this is how the Caislean burger should be eaten."

Tahlia climbed on the barstool. Her hands shook slightly as she reached for the burger, making him feel guilty for making her wait. She took a bite and closed her eyes.

"Oh God, it's so good." She licked her lips, snatching up a few hot fries.

Trick pushed the accompanying vanilla milkshake in front of her and backed away, pretending to fuss in the kitchen. He hadn't known the fridge was stocked with an assortment of pre-made meals, else he would have popped one of those in the oven to warm up. Snacks filled the cupboards, along with a wide range of soft drinks and teas.

Out of the corner of his eye, he watched her eat. Thinking him distracted, she attacked the food, biting and chewing so fast he was worried she might choke.

A slow anger bubbled in his gut. He masked it with effort. *Fuck.* How long had it been since she eaten a good meal?

"It wasn't that long," Tahlia said before taking a sip of her shake.

"What?"

"You asked how long it's been since I'd eaten."

He grimaced. "I meant to keep that in my head, sorry."

Tahlia shrugged. "I was working for a caterer at the end there. She did outreach and recruitment at a women's shelter I was staying at. I got excellent leftovers."

Leftovers, Christ. A woman like Tahlia deserved to be wined and dined at the best restaurants in the world, and she worked for scraps.

Not anymore. He was going to ply her with gourmet food until she regained the weight she'd lost living on the streets.

"Her name was Gina by the way. She's trying to get on your list of preferred vendors."

He blinked. "What?"

She inhaled a fry and frowned at her burger. "At the Caislean in Manhattan. She's trying to get on your preferred—"

He cut her off with a wave. "Is that what you were doing there? Were you working catering an event at *our* hotel when I bumped into you in New York?"

Tahlia nodded, taking another big bite. She gestured to the center of the patty with a frown. "What is this?"

"Foie gras," he answered absently. Inwardly, he was reeling. *She had been working at one of their hotels.* What were the chances? He didn't know how to calculate the odds, although it was a good bet she could.

"It's a small world," he said distantly, rocking on his heels before frowning at her. "Do you want something else to eat? I'm sorry I didn't think to ask if you liked goose liver. This kitchen is fully stocked. I can make you anything."

"No! This is amazing. I was just surprised at the unexpected mushiness. But it's a good mushy."

His lips quirked, but he found it difficult to smile. "Can you tell me more about the time you were missing?"

He'd lost weeks of sleep wondering what happened to her after the memorial service.

Her eyes grew distant. "It's not as bad as you think. Yes, there were scary moments and shitty people, but I met some nice ones, too. People in circumstances worse than mine. I got lucky one or two times."

He huffed aloud. Lucky was not the word he would use. "When?"

Maia told them about her family and how her father had been dead when she woke up in Florida.

She held up a finger. "Meeting Gina was one stroke of luck. She helped me."

Her eyes flared. "Oh no! I was supposed to meet her after the game. She doesn't know what happened to me. But I don't have a number for her—she never gave it to me because I don't have a phone. She would just leave messages for me at the shelter."

He picked up his phone. "Don't worry. I'll find her. If she catered an event for us, then my office will have her number."

Checking the time, he decided midnight wasn't too late, not for this. "Keep eating," he ordered.

Tahlia obeyed, her eyes tracking him as he dialed the manager at their Manhattan hotel. Satisfied she was going to finish everything and then some, he pulled out a half pint of vanilla bean ice cream from the freezer and set it in front of her to thaw.

"Kemper," he greeted the manager when he answered. "I need you to put me through to a vendor."

Gina the caterer was so relieved to hear his news, she cried over the phone.

"You don't have to worry about her anymore," Trick assured the woman as Tahlia danced in front of him, gesturing for him to pass the phone. He held up a finger, asking her to wait.

"I'm going to be keeping a close eye on her. Thank you for watching out for her. Consider your place on the preferred vendor list a lock."

He handed the handset over as a very loud squeal came over the speaker. Tahlia grinned, covering the speaker for a second. "You won't regret it. Gina's food is great."

Kemper agreed. He also found her reliable, which was why guaranteeing the coveted slot wasn't a hardship. Although, he'd have done something else for her if she was crap. Anyone who helped other women when they were down deserved a hand.

Tahlia talked, giving Gina a very abbreviated version of events. She didn't mention being stalked or even hurt, but something told him the savvy woman she was speaking to could read between the lines.

"I'm okay," Tahlia repeated for the third time, picking at the ice cream with a spoon he'd shoved at her. "Or I will be soon. Yes, I'll call you as soon as I know what I'm doing next."

Trick frowned at that last phrase. If Tahlia thought she was going back to catering in New York, she was crazy. He didn't get a chance to tell her that, though. A few minutes later, she was yawning, her lids growing heavy as she nodded in response to whatever Gina was saying.

He plucked the phone out of her hand when she glanced at him and jumped a little, as if she'd forgotten he was there. "Sorry, Gina. This one has to go to bed now."

"Well, don't you keep her up then," the woman scolded in shades of motherly reproach. "Seriously, take care of her."

"I intend to," he promised, ushering Tahlia up out of her seat as he hung up.

Trick helped Tahlia wash up, giving her another painkiller before helping her to the bed. She yawned again and was drifting off when she saw him reach for the buttons on his shirt.

"What are you doing?"

"I told myself if I found you, I wouldn't let you out of my sight. Now, you can kick me out if you want, but I'll just move to the couch in the living room. I won't be far."

She snorted as he took his shirt off. "What happened to me being able to lock you out of my room?"

"You can do that later—when you've healed and you really have something to worry about," he said, stripping down to his boxers.

Tahlia's mouth quirked as he climbed into the empty space next to her.

"This bed is big enough for me and five of you. You won't even know I'm here. So for now, rest. Regain your strength. If you need anything, just ask."

He took one of the many bed pillows and put it between them.

Tahlia picked it up and tossed it on the floor. "Get on my other side. It hurts less."

He complied, relaxing when she curled up against him. Several minutes passed in silence. Her deep and even breathing signaled she'd fallen asleep.

"I'm not going to let anyone hurt you," he whispered.

Trick didn't have a lot of practice destroying people, but for her, he could learn.

CHAPTER 18

It took over a week for Tahlia to stop jerking awake when the alarm on Patrick's watch beeped every morning. It wasn't always safe to doze in front of strangers, even at the shelters, so she'd developed the habit of sleeping lightly and waking early. Personal belongings had a way of disappearing when she wasn't watching, even in the safe places.

But the wide fluffy bed in the Caislean's penthouse suites soon worked its magic. She slept later and later, waking only briefly when Patrick would kiss her goodbye before going to his room to shower and change every morning.

Most of the week was spent in the suite as she slowly recovered her mobility. The doctor, Eric Tam, remarked on her quick recovery.

"I still want you to take it easy," he ordered as he left the day before. "And don't be afraid to take the codeine if you need it. Proper pain management is essential to the healing process. Nobody's going to let you get hooked on anything on my watch."

Tahlia promised, but truthfully didn't need the pills. She could take the mild discomfort of her injuries now that she could afford to rest.

Patrick had been wonderful since she arrived. He kept popping in to see her throughout the day, surprising her with little gifts or treats. He ate dinner with her every night and bought her a phone, so she could text him when he was working in his office.

Maia couldn't come to see her because of the doctor's imposed bedrest, but Tahlia was able to video chat her every other day.

Maggie Tyler and her best friend Peyton Carson also dropped by to check on her almost every day, up until Maggie had to leave town to help with a big conference at their Edinburgh hotel. Then Peyton came alone. As soon as she could walk, she insisted on giving Tahlia the grand tour.

"Don't tell Trick I busted you out today," Peyton told her, releasing them from the penthouse floor by putting her thumb to a space-age panel before pushing the lobby button.

Tahlia squinted at the sleek panel, remembering how impressed she'd been with it during her first trip up to the suite level with Patrick. Her family was notoriously technophobic. She hadn't even owned a cell phone until she moved to Boston for school.

Holding onto to the cane Dr. Tam provided to help her walk, she murmured her thanks for the tour. Though they hadn't spent that much time alone together before, Tahlia liked Peyton. From what Maia told her, they had some things in common regarding difficult childhoods.

"Patrick doesn't know about this outing?" she asked, half expecting him to round the corner.

Peyton grinned. "If he did, would he be chill, or would he insist on carrying you back to your suite right now?"

Tahlia tilted her head up to the security cameras in the corner of the elevator. "You have a point… let's not tell him. So where are we going?"

"I'm pretty sure Liam would join Trick in stringing me up if I took you down to the lobby level, but we can start at the mezzanine," Peyton said brightly. "It's where the spa and the hotel's five-star restaurant are. There's also a gym in the basement, but it's way too early for that judging from the cane. We can still take a tour, however, for future reference. It's a nice setup—there's a weight room, lap pool, and a sauna."

Tahlia smiled wistfully at the mention of the pool. "I don't have a bathing suit."

She didn't have much of anything. Maia's husband had generously taken charge of packing up her apartment when she'd been taken, but he'd put the lot in storage. As soon as her family learned about it, they'd sent a lawyer to make a claim to collect her belongings. Calen hadn't relented, claiming they were evidence, but the legal tangle meant she still didn't have her clothes.

Patrick told her to charge anything she needed from the hotel's luxury clothing shops to his account, but that was far too generous. For the moment, she was wearing clothes borrowed from Peyton and Maggie. Both were close to her size.

"Oh, I wouldn't worry about that. Trick will happily get you a bikini if you mention the pool." Peyton waggled her eyebrows, making her laugh.

"Something tells me I wouldn't want to wear anything he picked out." Her smile faded as wondered how she was going to pay for a whole new wardrobe.

"Are you okay?" Peyton asked, holding open the door for the spa.

She shrugged, flicking her eyes over the well-appointment reception desk area of the spa. The walls were white and with light ocean-blue accents. Soothing music tinkled in the background. A welcome area with couches and sofas was to the left, while a grand display of the hotel's skin care line filled multiple shelves on the right.

"Um, Peyton. I don't think I can afford anything here," she said in a low voice, her eyes widening at the prices on the spa menu the other woman handed her.

"It's on the house."

Tahlia shook her head, tensing. "I don't want Patrick to have to pay for this. It's bad enough I'm crashing in that ridiculous suite without paying."

Her family had money, but they hadn't supported her going off to school, so she'd lived exclusively on her graduate student stipend. The small salary paid for her apartment and basic living expenses, but little else. Budgeting had been essential.

"Tahlia, don't be silly. Everyone needs a little help sometimes. If you want a facial or a manicure, you can use my employee code. Everyone on the staff is entitled to a free service once a year, based on seniority—including the maids and cleaning staff. I've been working here since this place opened so I have credits stocked up. I never have time to use them. But now you're here, we can both get something done. A massage is probably a bad idea given the injuries to your ribs, but we could get a facial or a haircut. Georgina is an artist with her shears."

Tears stung at her eyes at Peyton's generosity. Aside from Maia, she didn't have very many real friends. She didn't know what to do when people were kind.

Peyton noticed her rapid blinking. "Why don't we schedule something after we've done the whole circuit?" she suggested brightly, glossing over the uncomfortable scene.

After waving to the attendant at the desk, Peyton ushered her though the warren of spa rooms, showing her everything from the facial rooms to the hamam-style sauna and mud baths.

Each member of the staff greeted her by name. "Everyone is so...warm," Tahlia observed after a particularly effusive maid stopped them in the hall to gently hug her and wish her a speedy recovery before reminding Peyton to eat.

"Most of the staff in this hotel have been with the Tylers for years. That one, Constanza, worked for their parents at their old B&B. She's like one of their four unofficial moms. She's kind of one for me, too, I guess. I've known Maggie since grade school. The B&B was like a second home."

They were passing through the tearoom, where an English tea service was available to guests from morning until dinner. Peyton snagged a puff pastry from a loaded table and pressed another on her.

"They lost their mom fairly young, didn't they?" Tahlia asked as the other woman munched away.

Peyton swallowed with a distant nod. "Both parents at once. It was a car crash. Maggie and I were still in elementary school. Liam was a senior, and Trick was a freshman in high school. Relatives wanted to split them up when it happened, but Liam fought them off. He insisted the family stay together. The small B&B staff pitched in to make sure they were able to. Since then, they've all been absorbed into the upper echelons of the hotel chain."

She gestured to their surroundings. "After Liam and Trick opened this place, that loyal crew received a huge pay bump and excellent retirement accounts. The Tylers take care of their own."

It was mind-bending how young Patrick and his brother had been when they founded their hotel chain. "Liam and Patrick must be amazing businessmen to have built all this."

"They are. Liam's brutal in the boardroom and Maggie's no slouch either. Trick acts like the soft touch, more devil-may-care, but in reality, he's a born salesman. He could sell anything. He's almost better at that than poker, although since you beat him, that probably doesn't mean much to you," Peyton teased.

Did he tell everyone? "It was only one game. Maybe I got lucky," she offered.

Peyton's lips quirked. "Did you?"

Tahlia's shoulders dropped. "No. I'm better."

The other woman's peal of laughter preceded them into the restaurant, where the chef personally served them lunch. The sommelier also fussed over them until Peyton sent him away, telling him Tahlia couldn't drink with the painkillers she was on.

"That was delicious," she said as they resumed their tour.

"All the food here is amazing," Peyton boasted, leading the way to the elevators.

Their next stop was the manager's office, located directly behind the main desk.

"I thought I wasn't allowed on the lobby floor yet."

Peyton waved that away. "As long as you're not in the open, we should be fine. Plus, this is my domain." She threw open a door, revealing a high-tech space filled with monitors.

Two men in dark suits nodded at them as Peyton shooed her to an intimidating semi-circular desk. Three huge monitors faced the leather rolling chair like some sort of space command center.

Peyton pulled up an extra chair for her to sit in. "This place doubles as security and our IT department. Kevin and Sam over there keep watch on all the floors and entrances via our internal camera feeds. I'm part of a team that maintains all the hotel's computers and encrypted Wi-Fi system."

Tahlia whistled, squinting at the command line interface on the closest screen. Her math skills didn't translate to being adept with computer languages. She knew the basics, of course, but Peyton must have been a very good programmer to make all this run.

The other girl typed a few commands on her keyboard, bringing up closed-circuit feeds from the penthouse floor. The men were in the reception area just outside of their offices, deep in conversation with a small group.

"Trick is done with his meeting, so we can expect him to start hunting you down soon."

"I don't mind if he finds me," Tahlia said, feeling like a voyeur as she watched him shake hands with another man on the monitor. In the background, Liam Tyler was standing with his assistant.

The Tylers oldest brother had dropped by her room the day before. Though he'd been polite and welcoming, his clipped speech and bear-like build intimidated her. She found it difficult to speak to him. Patrick was the complete opposite.

Peyton giggled. "Of course you don't mind. You're almost healed up. Soon, it will be time for *bam chicka wah wah.*"

Tahlia's ears heated. She jerked in the swivel chair to see if the two security men overheard.

"They are wearing earpieces, tuned to the in-house band. You could drive a truck in here and they wouldn't notice."

Chagrined, Tahlia turned back to her. "Patrick said he wants to take it slow," she confessed. "I wasn't sure I did, but it's a good idea. I don't have a whole lot of experience with men. My family never allowed any near me—even after I left home."

Despite the distance, her relatives kept up a relentless surveillance. Every time a man showed more than a passing interest in her, she received a warning, usually in the form of a phone call from her father. She was repeatedly warned to discourage suitors, so that was what she did, albeit as subtly as she could. If that didn't work, her cousins would start appearing in the same places until Tahlia was forced to be more direct with the man in question.

She gave herself a little shake. "I don't know why I'm telling you this. You're like Patrick in a way. It's far too easy to tell you things I shouldn't."

Peyton beamed. "It's a gift. Rest assured, whatever you tell me, I will keep to myself. Ask Maggie when she gets back. I'm a vault." She gripped Tahlia's hand before letting go to scribble on a post-it. "If you need anything or if the guys get too overbearing, call me. This is my extension. It will forward to my cell phone if I'm walking the halls."

Tahlia mumbled her thanks, her throat tight with emotion. She tucked the post-it into a pocket. "I don't know how I ended up here. It almost doesn't seem real, having so many people concerned for my welfare."

Peyton tilted her head contemplatively. "Actually…now that you mention it, caring about women in distress is kind of our thing."

Puzzled, Tahlia raised an eyebrow.

"I can show you." Peyton stood. "Come with me."

She led her to a large storage closet across the room. As soon as they crossed the threshold, a motion sensor turned the lights on.

"What is this?" She was staring at shelf after shelf full of toys.

Tahlia picked up a small brown teddy bear from the nearest one. It was one of dozens in different colors. There were also trucks and dolls, a few handheld video games, and lots of books. On the other side of the room was another shelf stocked with nondescript black backpacks. Each appeared to be filled.

"These supplies are for our special gold shield rooms. At every Caislean hotel, the reservation desk holds back a couple of rooms for women in difficult circumstances. Most of them are leaving an abusive boyfriend or husband. They're referred to the hotel by their local domestic abuse hotline when the circumstances are extreme enough. It's usually when they don't have room at the local shelter, or their partner poses too high a risk for that to be a safe option."

She indicated the bear Tahlia was holding. "It was Trick's idea to keep new toys on hand. When they run, it's often a woman with small kids. Often, they're forced to leave everything behind. It happened so frequently Trick started stashing toys in his office. Eventually, we got organized and set up this closet. The backpacks are for the moms. Each is filled with toiletries, underclothes, a t-shirt, and track pants. There's even a preloaded disposable cell phone in there."

"Wow." Tahlia blinked as a sudden thought occurred to her. "Does Liam know?"

Peyton's grin was wry. "Everyone always asks that. They assume, and I don't blame them, that because he's such a bottom-line kind of guy that he either doesn't know or puts up with it because Maggie and Trick teamed up on him."

She settled against a shelf and crossed her arms. "Let me tell you a story. A couple of years ago, a new hotshot assistant manager started here. It was a busy conference week. The holidays were approaching, so the hotel was at capacity. This guy had been warned that the gold shield rooms were off limits, but both Trick and Maggie happened to be out of town overseeing events at other hotels. The new guy thought he was being smart by renting out the rooms. He thought Liam would approve—right up until we got a call that a woman and her daughter needed a place to stay and it was an emergency."

"Wow. What happened?"

Peyton leaned in. "Her psycho ex was right on their heels. One of the supply vans went to pick them up, only for us to discover the rooms had been rented out. Not five minutes later, Liam was down in the main office tearing the guy a new one. They could hear him yelling all the way down to the kitchens. That manager never made the same mistake again. No one does."

She broke off and pointed to the backpacks. "Those were actually Liam's idea. Trick is great at figuring out ways to help, but he's not detail-oriented. Liam's the practical one. He's the one who realized a woman in those circumstances probably needs an extra pair of clean underclothes. Liam is also the one who makes sure the toys are reordered when we run low. Trick sometimes forgets. Liam doesn't ever mention it of course. The one time I thanked him for doing it, he looked at me as if I were crazy. Then he told me not to bother him unless it was an emergency." She sniffed. "He's at his rudest when you're trying to be nice to him."

Tahlia felt terrible. "I'm sorry I misjudged him."

"Oh, don't be." Peyton laughed. "Most of the time Liam deserves to be judged. He can be an ass."

Her friend's bright demeanor didn't last. When they went back to Peyton's control center, the video feed showed Liam in close conversation to a woman in a tight tailored skirt suit. The elegantly coiffed stranger was touching his chest possessively.

All the light faded from Peyton's face.

The change was so dramatic, Tahlia knew something was wrong. "Who is that?" she asked softly.

Peyton turned away, shutting off the feeds before filling her screen with a series of commands Tahlia couldn't make sense of.

"Her name is Caroline Wentworth. Her father owns a small boutique chain. She and Liam see each other on and off. Mostly on, recently."

"Oh." Tahlia didn't know what to say.

Maia had once mentioned something over coffee one day at work. *Peyton only has eyes for one man, and he is the only one who doesn't know how she feels.*

That conversation had taken place after they all met for drinks one night, right after Peyton tossed the number of a hot guy who'd hit on her into a street bin.

Maia hadn't mentioned any names, but Tahlia guessed she knew what it was now.

"I don't suppose you want to go up to the tearoom and get a scone?" She wasn't hungry, but anything seemed preferable to staying here where Peyton could watch the man she loved with another woman in a few keystrokes.

"I think you're going to be busy." Peyton's eyes were shiny, but she made a half-hearted effort at smiling.

Tahlia followed the other girl's gaze to see Patrick entering the security room.

She took a moment to admire how well his tall, muscled form filled out his blue suit.

Dear Lord, I'm actually salivating. She hurriedly turned back to Peyton.

The other woman nudged her lightly. "Don't worry. Now that you're staying here, I'm sure we'll get many chances to hang out."

"Okay, if you're sure. Unless you want to go get a manicure now—Patrick won't mind if we hit the spa, do you?" she asked as he joined them.

"No, go on with Trick," Peyton replied, an amused glint returning to her eye. "I suppose I should try and get a little work done," she added airily.

"That's what we pay you the medium bucks for." Trick grinned at her before offering Tahlia his arm. She took it instead of the cane, turning back to Peyton when they reached the door.

Tahlia couldn't be sure given the distance, but it appeared a corner of one of Peyton's screens was back on the reception feed from the penthouse offices.

CHAPTER 19

Trick ushered Tahlia back into his suite with a hand on the small of her back. She set the cane down against the couch with a stiff smile.

"When you said you wanted to play cards I assumed you meant next door."

"We can go there if you want," he said, gesturing to the adjoining door. "But all my fresh decks are here. Why don't I grab one and we can switch?"

"Oh, it's okay," Tahlia said, her cheeks a deep pink. She turned away, her finger trailing along the back of the sofa as she walked to the windows.

He studied her averted eyes with a pang in his chest. "Is something wrong?"

Tahlia dipped her head and stayed quiet.

Trick hid his disappointment. After spending every free moment with her this week, he believed she'd grown comfortable around him. They'd cuddled on the couch watching television and talked for hours after sharing gourmet meals in the dining alcove. Why was she so hesitant with him now?

She cleared her throat. "I feel better, but I'm having a hard time. You see, I really want to be with you..."

Oh.

"I want that, too," he said slowly. "But we can take as long as you need," he added with as much conviction as he could muster.

Truthfully, waiting was hellish for him. Being close to her while keeping the intensity of his desire in check had been a challenge. In his youth, Trick hadn't practiced much self-restraint when it came to women. Discretion—yes. While he'd played fast and loose in his teens and early twenties, after the success of the hotel, he'd been forced to be more discerning about the women he socialized with.

Making bank with the hotel chain put a target on his back, more so than his brother. As the more easygoing of the pair, he was the one in the crosshairs of every gold-digger in Manhattan. Consequently, he'd been forced to be more careful. Nevertheless, when he wanted a companion, ladies in his sphere were ready and willing.

With Tahlia, he needed to tread carefully. His desire for her was an order of magnitude greater than anything he'd felt before.

The subject of this earthshaking hunger was picking at her nails. "That's not exactly what I mean. I *want* to be close to you. It's just...I won't know what to do."

Wait. Was she telling him what he thought she was telling him? If so, this was going to require some tactful ingenuity. He wanted her to be comfortable taking the next step.

Inspiration struck as he caught sight of the stack of sealed decks on his bookshelf.

"I have an idea," he said, taking one down. He walked to the dining table and wagged his fingers at her.

"What are we doing?"

His smile grew devilish. "Strip poker."

Tahlia laughed aloud. "Seriously? Aren't you afraid of getting whipped again?"

Trick waggled his eyebrows. "Oh, I'm comfortable in my skin. But what makes you think you're going to win this time? I've played in every major casino in this hemisphere against players of all stripes—including one or two legends. I think my odds are pretty good."

"All right, then. If you're sure…" Tahlia sat at the table, holding her hand out for the deck.

A half hour later, he was naked except for a single vicuna sock —which he'd chosen to wear someplace other than his foot.

The game started well enough for him. He'd won the first hand.

Blushing a rosy pink, Tahlia's eyes widened when she saw his cards.

"Why don't you start with your shoe?" he suggested.

She tittered nervously and toed off one of the sneakers Peyton lent her. "Don't get too cocky. It's only a shoe."

He grinned unrepentantly, shuffling and dealing by rote. "Be prepared to lose the other one. I'm coming after that sock, too."

"Really?" she asked, a corner of her mouth lifted.

"Oh, yeah."

Lifting her cards, the amused expression on her face melted away to nothing. Poker face securely on, she dropped two cards on the table, which he quickly replaced.

She won with three of a kind. He removed his tie with a flourish, tossing it aside the way a stripper would.

Two pair. His left shoe, which was quickly followed by the right.

"Are you sure you're not throwing this game?" Tahlia asked when a straight cost him his shirt.

"Nope." He laughed, glad he'd kept up his sparring routine with Liam this week. His pecs were as defined as they were ever going to get. He wanted to be at his best around her.

"My goal was to get both of us undressed. Or, if I'm being honest, just you."

Tahlia snorted. "How's that plan working out?"

"Not good," he admitted.

She hummed, taking his pants with the next hand. By the time she laid down a flush against his three of a kind, he was down to his boxers and the sock.

Well, this hasn't gone as planned. But Trick wouldn't be Trick if he didn't make the best of the situation.

Time to go big or go home.

"Feel free to close your eyes," he teased, still incredulous at how badly this had gone for him.

Trick stood and turned his back. He peeked over his shoulder with a wink as he slowly dragged the waistband of his shorts down, exposing his pale ass.

He wiggled. "You might not want to stare directly at this. I skipped the run to Turks and Caicos this year, so this area hasn't gotten a lot of sun. There's a chance you might be blinded by my extreme paleness. But I am toned, something that might be better demonstrated by feel," he joked, flexing his glutes as he surreptitiously replaced the shorts with the sock.

He rose, mimicking the exaggerated bend and snap Reese Witherspoon popularized in one of her movies—hand movements included.

Tahlia's laughter was so loud he didn't hear the door opening.

"What the hell are you doing?" Liam asked.

Trick whirled. His brother was standing in the open doorway, a sheath of papers in one hand and his phone in the other.

Crap.

"He's losing at strip poker," Tahlia offered helpfully.

Liam's habitual scowl faded as he broke into an ear-to-ear grin. "You're losing *again?*"

He lifted his phone and quickly snapped a pic. "Calen has to see this," he chortled.

"Hey asshole, don't even think about it!" Trick hurried to the couch. He clutched one of the throw pillows in front of him, tossing another at his brother's head.

Liam batted it away, tossing the papers on the nearest chair. "Sign those before tomorrow. They go out first thing in the morning."

He was gone before Trick could think of a sufficiently acerbic comeback. When he turned back to the table, it was empty and the connecting door was standing open.

CALM DOWN, Tahlia ordered herself sternly. She'd been caught up in Trick's lighthearted game just now, but the minute Liam walked in on them, it was as if she'd been doused with cold water.

You need to get over this. She was allowed to have a life. There was no one stopping her anymore. *Except you.*

Rubbing her arms, she shifted to the window. The sun was starting to go down, but the lights in the neighboring high-rises were already turning on.

"Tahlia?"

Patrick was standing at the door of her bedroom, a pillow the only thing keeping his privates private.

Her eyes widened as he dropped the pillow, pulling off the sock he'd jokingly placed there. His face deadly serious, he walked toward her.

Breath quickening, Tahlia retreated instinctively, jumping when her back hit the cold glass of the window.

Patrick didn't stop until he was standing right in front of her. He wasn't wearing a stitch, but nothing in his manner betrayed the slightest hint of awkwardness.

Of course, he had nothing to be embarrassed about. His long lean form was nothing short of glorious. He wasn't as bulky like his brother, but every muscle in his arms and chest was perfect and defined. It was as if he'd been carved by an obsessive-compulsive sculptor. Every line of him was right where it was supposed to be, nothing superfluous, nothing in excess. His body was spare and flawless.

Well, not everything is spare. She blushed, averting her eyes from his proudly jutting cock.

Patrick's chiseled arms settled on either side of her, effectively trapping her against the glass.

"How did I lose the upper hand here?" she marveled, almost to herself.

He was the one standing there with nothing but a smile. How was it that *she* felt exposed?

His grin was pure sin. "Well, I know one way we can get back on an even footing."

He knelt to untie her shoe, before going for the waistband of her borrowed jeans. His hands skimmed down the sensitive skin of her thighs, sending tingles all the way down to her ankles.

Tahlia stepped out her pants, her heart racing. Patrick guided her arms, until she was wrapping them around his neck. They whirled, and she was suddenly on the bed, pinned underneath all his rough satin heat.

Her top and bra melted away. Dressed in only her panties, she trembled as his fiery openmouthed kiss wiped her brain of coherent thought.

Her body burned as skin met skin. Trick stroked and teased, nibbling all along her neck until she was seething and writhing under his touch.

Nothing she'd ever experienced came close to this. Her hands shook as she explored his chest, running her fingers over his six-pack and the unreal little cleft at his hips. No magazine fitness model could match him.

"I love how wet you are," Patrick said in her ear, sucking the delicate lobe into his mouth as his hand drifted to trace the seam between her legs.

Shuddering, Tahlia pressed against his hand, awkwardly trying to satisfy the unfamiliar hunger clawing at her. The foreign drumbeat of lust made her heart race. She ran her hands over the taut muscles of his back, pressing him closer with a whimper.

"Shh..." Patrick soothed, his tongue darting out to lick her lips. "I'm going to take care of you, Ace."

He lifted his head, his eyes black with desire. "I don't suppose there's any way you're on the pill?"

"N-no."

Trick rolled over, exposing her heated body to the cool air. He stood over her, taking a foil packet out of his pant pocket. She watched with parted lips as he rolled the condom on impatiently, before crawling back on the bed like a hungry predator.

He put his lips to her bare breast, sucking her nipple into his mouth. He lathed the tip, making her cry out and arch before moving his attention to the other one. His hand gripped her hips, pulling down her panties in one smooth move.

"Open your legs for me, baby," he whispered against her mouth.

Returning his kiss, she tremulously obeyed, gasping when he settled against her before slowly sliding down.

Tahlia's eyes fluttered closed as he bent, his mouth moving over her most intimate flesh. He licked and gently bit, using his hands to open her.

Her nipples pebbled as her hips began to rise and fall in time with his rhythm. Hot and flushed, she squirmed, forcing him to hold her down. She lost all sense of time, transforming into a creature of pure sensation.

"Look at me."

Her eyes flew open to meet Patrick's eyes.

"No, I meant there. Look at me *there*."

"*Oh*."

Giggling nonsensically, Tahlia tilted her head. Though sheathed, his cock was rigid, rubbing against her pussy with teasing little strokes. Each movement sent a shock of pleasure pulsing through her.

"What do I do?" she whispered. Tahlia may have been a superior poker player, but here she was the novice.

"Wrap your legs around me." Patrick fitted himself at her opening, pushing inside with a grim determination lining his face.

"You're so wet this shouldn't hurt that much," he added, pressing a soft kiss to her lips.

He was wrong. A different kind of burning consumed her as he flexed his hips, fighting the resistance of her untried body. Tahlia's lips parted, her breath growing short as he drove his cock until he was flush to the hilt.

Her mouth gaped, shocked at the alien sensation. With no basis of comparison, she didn't know if Trick was truly over-endowed, but his long, thick length filled her to capacity and slightly beyond.

"Are you okay?" Patrick's voice was hoarse, his breathing as ragged as hers.

"I don't know. You don't seem to fit," she said, wincing a little as he shifted minutely.

"No, baby. I fit perfectly. You'll get used to me…starting now." Trick's hand moved down, kneading her clit with a sure rhythmic motion.

Underneath him, she jerked, electricity shooting through her. Patrick hissed as she clenched down on him. "I'm going to move now, baby. If it doesn't get better, tell me to stop. Keep watching me."

His hips lifted, retreating only a few inches before pushing back in. Then he did it again and again, until he was thrusting in and out at a steady rate.

The pain receded. She was still a bit sore, but there was another sensation now—almost as if he were tickling her. It wasn't unpleasant.

Feeling warmer now, she moved her legs experimentally, tightening them around him. Almost instantly, the tickling became a ripple of pleasure as his cock hit a spot deep in her channel.

A moan rose from deep in her throat. She flexed her hips, her hands clutching at his shoulders.

"That's it, Ace, sing for me." Patrick's voice wasn't soft anymore. It was clipped and a little hard, which matched his pace as he quickened his thrusts.

She thought it would start hurting again, but each time his body met hers, she felt a pulse of heat. Each stroke built the pleasure, making her seethe and moan. She felt like a bowstring tightening, any moment she was going to break.

"Oh God, Patrick," she panted, squirming uncontrollably as she wrapped her arms around his chest, clawing his back inadvertently as she began to lose control.

Her eyes were glued to him. She couldn't tear her eyes away as his cock entered, pushing deep and then back out again. Each time he did, her body responded, pulsing as if clamoring for more.

He didn't answer, but she could sense his satisfaction. It was in the way he kissed her, pressing his lips to her hairline as his body took and plundered, staking a primal claim she could feel in her blood.

Tahlia forgot all about the long lonely years of sexual repression in a burning flash of sensuality. She rocked in time to Patrick's thrusts, glorying in his warmth and the rough silk of his skin. Heart beating in time to their rhythm, she ground against him, trying to bring them close enough to meld into each other.

It wasn't soft. It wasn't sweet. She was as hungry and as

wickedly greedy as the man possessing her, both straining to satisfy a hunger months in the making.

The explosion came without warning. Her body seized, clamping down tight on Patrick's as the violent spasms splintered her senses. She clung to him as he swore, pumping hard and fast, grinding against her. He let go with a shout, totally free and abandoned as liquid warmth flooded her pussy.

He collapsed over her, a sheen covering his heaving chest. A few short pants later, he rolled, taking her with him. She landed on his chest, still intimately connected to him.

"Holy heavenly *shit*," he muttered before turning to her. "Are you all right?"

Tahlia could still hear her heartbeat. It was almost thrumming loud enough to drown out his voice. "I think you killed me."

"You're kidding, right?" He laughed, still panting. "I thought you were supposed to be a novice. A rank amateur—and you destroyed me." Sobering, he ran his fingers over her hair. "I didn't hurt you, did I?"

She took stock before answering. There was a slight burning in her sheath, but overall, she felt great. This pleasant lethargy was new. *Is this what people referred to as being spent?*

"I'm a little sore, but nothing of note." A smile teased her lips. Patrick was glowing with sweat, and he wore a slightly dazed expression. "So I did well?"

Patrick's hand tightened into a fist in her hair. "Let's put it this way...I'm never letting you go."

Tahlia shivered, but for the first time in a while, she wasn't afraid.

The feeling wouldn't last.

CHAPTER 20

I rushed her.

Trick studied Tahlia all through breakfast. She was distracted, staring off into space. Twice, she stopped eating, the fork halfway to her mouth.

Damn it. This wasn't how this was supposed to go. Watching Tahlia discover the pleasure of sex, getting to be the one to teach her, made for an amazing week, the very best of his life. But while she certainly enjoyed everything they did, Tahlia was sometimes downcast after. And he'd been too much of a coward to ask why.

It will be okay. If she were having second thoughts about him, he'd just have to give her third thoughts until she was where he was.

For the first time in his life, Trick was in love. He'd known for a while, but he had yet to say it aloud. That was probably a good thing. If she was feeling skittish, telling her the truth might terrify her.

The fork paused a third time. Trick put his hand on Tahlia's wrist, urging her to put the fork down. "Ace, tell me what's wrong."

Her lashes flickered. "Nothing."

Trick's lips tightened. Pulling his chair closer to her, he held her hand in both of his. "Tahlia, I know things have gone a little fast for us. You must be overwhelmed. If you want to slow things down..." He gritted his teeth. "Then I'm fine with that."

He hoped she wouldn't call him out for lying.

Tahlia squeezed his hand and gave him a bracing smile. "That's not it."

"Then it's your family," he decided.

She sighed, silently confirming his second guess was the correct one. "You don't have to worry about them anymore. You're safe here. I know it's a little rough being cooped up all the time, but that won't last forever. And if it takes longer than we want, and you get sick of this view, we'll hop on the company jet and I'll give you another one. Or we can sneak away to Vegas or Monte Carlo. You can beat the pants off me at a real casino."

Tahlia leaned back in her chair. "I'm not worried about me. Or rather, I'm so used to worrying about myself, it's basically just background noise in the back of my brain now."

"So what's wrong?"

"You."

A punch to the groin couldn't have hurt more.

"No, not like that." Tahlia stood and rushed over to him, climbing into his lap, her arms squeezing him hard around the neck. "I'm worried about you."

She leaned back to meet his eyes. "I was never allowed to be close to anyone—not even members of my own family. I was always kept separate. They watched me like a hawk. If I even got close to anyone, they would scare them away, even after I left for school. I could never have a relationship under those circumstances. I don't know what they'll do when they find out about you."

"Is that what this is all about?" Trick couldn't decide if he was relieved or not. "Tahlia, I can take care of myself. You're the one we need to protect."

She gave him pitying glance. "Patrick, there is no doubt in my mind that if they could, they would hurt you—or worse. They might try to kill you out of spite for helping, let alone being involved with me. I would put nothing past them."

His hands rubbed her back. "I am being careful, and this threat won't last forever. Trust me."

Her expression didn't clear. She pursed her lips, her eyes darker than their usual silver blue. "I do trust you. But don't underestimate them. You can't fight crazy."

There was more she wasn't saying, but he didn't want to press her. Though they hadn't been together long, he'd already learned that questioning Tahlia was the least effective way to get her to open it. It was better to wait and gently nudge.

His patience was slowly being rewarded. Though she hadn't told him much about her extended family, he'd learned she had a stepmother and younger brother, but both died when she was young. He'd tried to coax more out of her, but the only person she wanted to talk about was the housekeeper slash nanny who raised her.

"If it hadn't been for Ama, I'd have never learned anything about the world," she'd told him in bed one night. "She let me watch soap operas in her bedroom off the kitchen. Between her and the television, I learned the basics of just about everything—reading, cooking, cards. Ama showed me how to take care of myself."

"What happened to her?" he asked.

"I don't know." The desolate note in her voice nearly broke his heart. "My father told me she went back home to Cuba. But it was shortly after child protective services showed up. Someone had reported the fact I wasn't in school, and I wasn't registered for home education with the state so they came to investigate.

Afterward, my father hired a tutor for me. I wanted to go to school, so I was secretly thrilled. At least up until Ama disappeared."

Trick tightened his hold on her, pulling her waist until she was pressed against him in the bed. "When was this?"

Her head tilted back. "I think I was nine or ten. I just woke up one day and Ama wasn't there."

Seeing her now, with all her success in school, Trick could hardly believe her formal education began so late. From half-hearted homeschooling to a math degree from Harvard… Somehow, Tahlia more than made up for the time lost.

Of course, her housekeeper probably had a lot to do with that. Despite her position as a domestic, this Ama woman had given Tahlia the grounding she needed to overcome her sad and peculiar childhood. Some of the staff at the hotel did the same for him and Maggie after they lost their parents.

Trick made a mental note to try to discover what happened to the poor woman. If it was bad—if she ended up like Tahlia's dad—well, then, there was no reason to tell her the truth. But maybe he'd get lucky.

I might find the old woman alive and well in Cuba. Stranger things had happened.

TAHLIA HUGGED HER PH.D. ADVISOR, trying not to cry.

She was going to get her degree. Since she'd missed so much school, Tahlia assumed her dreams of a doctorate in Mathematics were over. But Patrick insisted on investigating the matter. He had invited her advisor, Dr. Karen Sattler, over for dinner.

Though they had a cordial working relationship, Tahlia was unprepared for the tears Dr. Sattler shed at seeing her alive and well.

"I'm so sorry I worried you," she said, a lump in her throat, as Dr. Sattler openly wept on her shoulder.

Patrick and Liam, who were both in attendance, stared at each other as if they didn't know what to do.

"It's not your fault, my dear," Dr. Sattler said, patting her grey hair in an effort to pull herself together. "I've been interviewed by those nice FBI officers. I know a little about what you've been facing, and I don't blame you for not getting in touch." She wiped her eyes, her sniff more disdainful than pained.

"And after speaking to some of your heinous relations, I can only wish you luck."

Tahlia could feel the blood draining from her face. "You've spoken to them?"

"Yes, your uncle Lucas and his attorneys called me several times," Dr. Sattler said with a shudder.

"What did he want?" Patrick frowned darkly.

He looks a lot more like Liam when he does that, Tahlia observed.

"He was trying to find out if I knew where she was, of course," Dr. Sattler said, sitting down on at the table with the upright carriage and British stiff upper lip Tahlia remembered her for.

Trick came up behind her, wrapping his arms around her waist as the older woman continued.

"I was glad I couldn't tell him anything. That man set my teeth on edge over the phone." Dr. Sattler's thin lips were almost a nonexistent seam. "He was all sweetness and light at first. He said he wanted to discuss your work in an effort to be close to you. But then he repeatedly tried to order me to call him if I heard anything about you, I reported him to campus security for harassment. After that, I only heard from his attorney."

Tahlia sat in stunned silence. Suddenly, she was cold, her fingers icy.

"I had no idea he'd reached out to you," she said in a hoarse voice.

Trick exchanged another loaded glance with his brother. She could practically see them flexing their muscles as if they were girding themselves for battle.

She wondered how many others Lucas reached out to. Dr. Sattler was no fool, but for many other people, she knew it would have been easy for Lucas to pass off his aggressive behavior as concern for his missing niece.

Still uneasy, she lapsed into silence, letting Patrick and Liam monopolize the conversation. They effortlessly soothed Dr. Sattler's jangled nerves, deftly steering talk back to the possibility of finishing her doctorate.

"It's not going to be a problem," her advisor assured her between bites of a delicious seafood risotto. "You've done so much good work toward the degree. A few more passes of the manuscript might be in order before we submit it to your committee for approval, but I think it would be a formality at this point."

"That's great news." Trick beamed at her, reaching over to squeeze Tahlia's hand.

She returned his smile, but the effort was hollow. Mention of her uncle had soured the evening.

Her work at Harvard had always been her safe space. No one in her family, aside from her father, ever asked about her research. And he hadn't wanted to hear the details. All he'd cared about was that she excelled, not so much what she excelled in. Just knowing Lucas asked about her work made it seem sordid. She knew her reaction was irrational, but she couldn't seem to help herself.

Patrick's brother cleared his throat. "Once everything is official, you should talk with our HR department. We can always find a place for talented people."

"Oh, leave her alone." Patrick threw a napkin at him. "Tahlia's degree is in crazy high-level math, not hotel hospitality. Stop trying to recruit my girlfriend."

"Why?" Liam asked bluntly. "I think she would be a great asset. She could do so many things in the organization."

"We already under-utilize great talent, or have you forgotten how bored Peyton's been lately?" Trick asked, serving her more wine.

"If Peyton wants more to do, all she has to do is ask," Liam grumbled in the gravel-filled bear voice he reserved for discussing their IT superstar.

"I'm just saying Tahlia doesn't need you pressuring her. She should get a chance to explore all her options—think tanks and stuff like that."

Tahlia exchanged a smile with Dr. Sattler. "Sorry. All Trick knows about math careers, he learned from *Good Will Hunting*." She snickered, successfully pulled out of her melancholia by the brothers' banter.

"I'm nearly three times your age and I still get pigeonholed by that movie, too," Dr. Sattler said, making them all laugh.

Later that night, she was alone with Trick in his office. He sat at his desk as she walked along the wall behind him, trailing her fingers along the bottom edge of the framed pictures. They showcased each of the hotels in the Caislean chain.

Their original intention had been to have a drink on the hotel's rooftop garden, but a sudden spat of rainy snow nixed that plan. Now they were sharing a glass of cognac to chase the chill away.

"That's our hotel in Sydney," Patrick said as she paused to examine the dramatic skyline behind a grand six-story building. Part of the distinctive Sydney opera house gleamed behind it.

"You don't usually see the back of this building," she observed, taking a big sip of her drink. She closed her eyes as the liquor washed through her body, spreading its artificial liquid heat.

"We can see it in person from whatever angle you want. Just say the word."

A corner of her mouth lifted. She stepped closer, brushing her legs against his knees. The alcohol was making her limbs heavy, but not unpleasantly so. She rather liked how her skin tingled when she touched Patrick, a sensation magnified by the cognac.

The hungry heat in his eyes was at odds with the fact he hadn't moved to touch her since sitting down. Then she noticed something.

"Are you sitting on your hands?" Was he that cold?

He grinned. "Sometimes I just like looking at you. But my hands don't want to cooperate. They're itching to tear that dress off."

A blush crept up her body. Tahlia downed the rest of her cognac, wincing as it burned her throat.

"Sorry, it's the kind of drink you sip." Patrick laughed, patting her on the back when she coughed.

"Well, I need my hands free," she said, setting the glass down on the desk before climbing on his lap, pushing her back against his chest.

His desk was littered with personal photos. Next to pictures of him and his siblings was one of Patrick by himself at a poker table next to Maia's husband.

She picked it up with a smile. "You're so young here."

"It was my twenty-first birthday. I decided to spend it gambling, legally, for the first time."

"Was this taken in Las Vegas?"

He shook his head. "No. I decided that wasn't special enough for the big two-one. This is the Hotel Monte Carlo."

Tahlia snatched the picture up, her eyes devouring every detail.

Patrick took the frame. "I will take you there as soon as we're free to leave," he murmured, moving his hand to cup her face.

He kissed her deeply, his tongue breaching the seam of her lips.

Time slowed down as a liquid heat poured into her body. Her nipples puckered and peaked under the soft black jersey of her bodice.

Patrick was reaching for the hemline of her dress when someone began to pound on the door.

He swore under his breath, shifting so she was sitting more demurely as his brother-in-law and his partner Ethan came in. Both wore dark expressions. Something had happened.

"This better be good," Patrick growled, holding her fast when she tried to stand up.

"What's wrong?" she asked, a sinking feeling in her stomach. A scowling Ethan was nothing new, but Jason was wearing a near-identical expression on his face.

"We have a big fucking problem. The local Florida PD has issued a warrant for your arrest."

CHAPTER 21

Tahlia wrapped her arms tightly around her middle. The brief warmth from the cognac and Patrick's kiss had dissipated. She felt like a block of ice, despite his arms cradling her shoulders.

They were sitting on the sofa in his office across from his brother and the two agents in an impromptu war council.

Her mouth felt like sandpaper. She was still in disbelief at the accusation being made. "This is crazy. My father was dead when I woke up."

"Are you sure?" Ethan consulted his notes. "You told us you were drugged and weren't sure how long you'd been unconscious. Is it possible he died while you were in the house?"

"For God's sake, you know she didn't do this." Liam was incensed on her behalf.

Ethan rolled his eyes at him. "Of course I know that. But we have to start preparing a defense here. We need to know every detail those bastards might throw at us."

Every detail?

Tahlia felt her legs weaken, her mind throwing up the ghastly images from that morning. She'd fought so hard to forget them. She hadn't told the agents or Patrick the full story.

"This is pretty inflammatory stuff." Ethan's nose was wrinkled as he read over the papers in his hand. "They're saying she stabbed him and stole his money because he wanted her to move back to Florida and I quote, 'take her rightful place' in the family."

Tahlia shuddered at the thought of what Lucas might consider her rightful place to be to be. "I don't know how long he'd been dead, but I assumed it had been a while. The blood didn't seem fresh."

Jason leaned forward in his seat. "What color was it? Was it dry? Did you see a knife lying nearby?"

She forced herself to swallow. Her throat was threatening to close on her. "I didn't, but…it would have taken more than one."

"More than one what?"

"Knife."

Ethan cocked his head at her, his expression softening in sympathy. "Because of the amount of blood?"

She shook her head. "Because of the number of pieces."

Patrick's head jerked. "Pieces of what?"

Her hands fluttered to her throat. "Of the body."

The men stared at her. Liam's mouth was open. Ethan frowned. "You didn't mention that before."

She picked at her nails. "Because you didn't press me. I didn't want to talk about it. I didn't want to *think* about it."

Visibly shivering, she pressed closer to Patrick, trying to borrow some of his warmth.

Her hands shook as she gestured to the carpet in the recessed conversation nook. "We have a Persian carpet almost twice this size. His legs and arms were at opposite ends, and his torso was in the middle. His head was roughly over there, *looking* at me," she said, pointing to a spot behind Jason's chair with an unsteady finger.

"Jesus fucking Christ," Liam swore, getting up to pour himself a drink.

"Bring the bottle," Ethan ordered. Liam, usually abrasive with the other man, didn't say a word as he poured him and Jason refills.

"Why didn't you say anything before?" Patrick rubbed her back, his face tight. "Christ, I should have had a therapist come in and talk to you."

She dismissed that. "I don't think I could have talked to anyone else about their psycho rituals."

Jason perked up. "It was ritualistic?"

Tahlia leaned back to stare at the ceiling, attempting to clear her mind enough to recall all those details. "I think so. I mean, I don't have a clear image anymore. It's like my brain stopped working after I saw him, but in my memory, I see a design on the carpet underneath him. Not a pentagram, but some other symbol in a circle. But the—the pieces formed a star shape."

"There is nothing about dismemberment in this damn report." Ethan waved the papers.

"There's also no pictures, which is rather damning in a way, isn't it?" Jason pointed out. "A prominent businessman like him is murdered, supposedly of a simple stab wound, but there's not a single picture."

Ethan appeared to mull that over. "What you describe would have taken a lot of time. You were in Boston early that morning. Do you remember how high the sun was after you crawled out the office window?"

"It was high but not overhead. It climbed higher as I left the grounds."

He made a note on a pad. "So maybe late morning? Good."

Her brow creased. "Why is it good?"

"Because the time of death on this report says he died in the pre-dawn hours, somewhere closer to three or four AM. I'm assuming it's accurate, although the cause of death is obviously fake."

He riffled through the papers again, holding up one of the sheets, and then sniffed. "They don't know you have an alibi up until dawn," he said, gesturing with the paper in Patrick's direction.

Liam narrowed his eyes at them, but he didn't ask what Ethan meant. Had Patrick not told his brother the story of meeting in the lobby afterward?

His consideration and concern for her reputation was sweet, but Tahlia didn't care if Liam decided she was loose for going to Patrick's room that night if it gave her an alibi for murder.

"Assuming they filed a flight plan, that alone should be enough to clear you," Jason said. "But it doesn't hurt to have Trick and Juan make statements establishing your whereabouts, in case they pull a fast one and want to alter the time of death so it points the finger at you."

Ethan nodded in agreement. "In the meantime, we'll pull whatever strings we can to get the un-doctored police report and any crime-scene photos, assuming they exist. One good shot of the body should be enough to get them to back off. Juries can't picture a woman dismembering a body for a reason. It's not easy to take one apart. Most don't have the strength."

Tahlia flinched, and Ethan winced. "Sorry."

"It's okay," she mumbled, rubbing her head. It wasn't sore, but she felt numb from head to toe.

"Just so we're clear, we're ignoring this summons for her to turn herself in?" Liam asked.

"Damn straight," Patrick said, his hold on the back of her neck tightening.

Ethan and Jason stood. "We'll lay it out for BPD. They still owe us for that mess with Dawson."

Liam muttered something she couldn't quite catch, but the agents ignored him.

Tahlia watched them leave with a heavy heart.

"I'm so sorry to have dragged you all into this mess," she said.

Liam tsked and rose. "Don't you worry about that. We take care of our own."

With that, he left, leaving her and Patrick alone.

"He doesn't really mean that, does he?"

Though gruff, Liam seemed very protective of his brother and sister, and to a lesser extent Peyton. He couldn't be happy Tahlia was exposing them to such sordid, evil people.

"My brother's a stubborn butthead about a lot of things, but he never says anything he doesn't mean."

There was something in his voice that made her twist to meet his eyes. Patrick's expression was shuttered, his face all angles and planes.

I was worried about the wrong brother.

"Patrick?" she whispered, unable to keep the concern out of her voice.

His face didn't soften the way it normally did.

"Come with me." Rising, he took her hand, pulling her along until they were down the hall inside his suite. He tugged until she followed him into his bedroom.

He closed the door with a snap, stalking her with slow deliberation.

Tahlia could feel the change in the atmosphere. It was electric and intimidating. Suddenly, her lover seemed unfamiliar.

"Are you okay?" A tiny tremor betrayed her anxiety.

He put his hands on the back of her head. She waited, but he didn't say anything. His jaw flexed, and his hands fisted in her hair, pushing her toward him.

"No one is taking you from me. *No one.*"

His grip was unforgiving. It made her scalp burn, but she didn't care. Tahlia pressed against him, silently begging for more.

Patrick's breath was hard and fast, the dark fire in his eyes new and a little disturbing. She stood there frozen as he stripped her, almost ripping the dress off.

Tahlia was left in her bra and panties. She started to take her heels off, but Patrick gave her a sharp shake of his head. He pushed her on the bed, stripping his shirt and pants off. He was crawling over her before his shorts hit the floor.

She tried to help him remove her underclothes, but he wasn't having any of it. Excited, and still a little apprehensive, she held her tongue as he pulled the thin strips of black fabric from her body.

The matching dark heels dug into the pristine white coverlet. Tahlia closed her legs, waiting for a sign of what to do as she peeked at Patrick from under her lashes.

For a very long moment, he just watched her.

He kneeled in front of her, his gaze sweeping over her as if he were memorizing the lines of her body. Then he reached for a pillow, stripping the silk pillowcase from it and rolling it into a makeshift rope.

His hands grasped her arms, moving to hold both her wrists together over her head. His hands blurred as he deftly tied and knotted the pillowcase around them.

"Leave them there," he ordered in a raw voice.

Stomach fluttering, she nodded.

"Good girl," he murmured, running his hands over her hips.

Tahlia resisted the urge to close her eyes. For a man who spent so much time in an office, his hands were rough and strong. She loved the way they felt sliding over the satiny skin of her thighs and stomach.

Patrick palmed her breast, squeezing her nipples until they stung before lowering his head. He drew each into his mouth, lapping them with his tongue before sucking them hard enough to make her cry out.

Tahlia squirmed, her heels scrabbling for purchase on the bed. Patrick clucked his tongue, pulling her leg up to swat her ass cheek, before pushing it back until her legs were parted wide.

He stared at her pussy, running his fingers over the seam of her lips, parting them to tease and pinch her clit with the same relentless hunger. He hadn't even put his fingers inside her, but she was so wet, already pulsing under his touch.

Forgetting herself, she reached for him. *"Patrick."*

Her channel was clenching desperately. She wanted—no, *needed* —a deeper penetration.

"I said don't move them." He adjusted her hands, positioning them back over her head and holding them fast with one hand. He rested his weight on a forearm, moving to grasp to his member.

He pumped his cock a few times, the thick length shining with a bead of precum at the tip. Then he crawled up the bed until he was over her face.

"Open your mouth."

Her pussy muscles clenched as she obeyed, parting her lips. Patrick traced them with his cock before pushing the tip inside.

Tahlia's closed her eyes, savoring his musk and salty taste. She rolled her tongue over the tip, eliciting a groan from him. Warm and aroused, Tahlia tried to take him in deeper, but he wouldn't cooperate. He let her suck on the head of his cock, but nothing more.

She was almost disappointed when he backed away. His cock withdrew out of her mouth with an audible little pop.

Patrick was breathing fast, parting her legs with hard hands. He didn't say anything as he pressed the tip to the entrance of her channel, waiting a beat for her to stop him. When she didn't, he flexed, driving into her bare, his satiny hard cock filling her roughly.

He stopped when he was all the way in, closing his eyes as if savoring the feel of her. Without the barrier of the condom everything was more intense, her wet heat sliding and straining against his thick length.

Muscles screaming with tension, Tahlia writhed, silently begging for him to move.

"*Please,*" she whispered finally when he didn't.

"Please what?" His voice was little more than a growl.

"Please fuck me."

Patrick smiled, but it wasn't warm or comforting. It was too hungry for that. His hand fisted in her hair and he braced himself, withdrawing and plunging back inside.

Tahlia clenched, trying to hold him inside, but she was too wet. He pistoned back and forth, plunging deeper and deeper with each stroke.

Drunk on sensation, she whimpered, her bound arms helpless as he moved harder and faster. "You're mine, Tahlia. *All mine.*"

Her heart swelled, her skin catching fire as she took each brutal thrust, absorbing it hungrily and responding in kind. Her hips twisted and writhed, while her upper body rose to abrade her rock-hard nipples on his chest.

Their bodies met and parted greedily, shifting and twisting until they were rolling all over the bed. Trick took hold of her, turning until she was on top of him, her back to his front.

Panting, Tahlia thrust her hips back, her pussy caressing his cock as it worked in and out from underneath now. Patrick held her by her hair, using it to pin her in place as he pounded inside her. Their bodies were slick with sweat when his cock began to jerk, and he climaxed with a shout.

His orgasm triggered hers. Tahlia spasmed around him, taking everything he had to give with a mad desperation that frightened her. It was like hurtling through the air at a thousand miles an hour, but she trusted him enough to surrender, exploding and coming with a keening wail.

They came down slowly. Tahlia clung to Patrick, all thought blotted from her mind.

For that, she was grateful.

CHAPTER 22

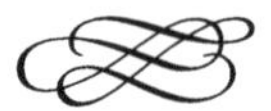

Trick nodded absently as Gene, Caroline Wentworth's father, continued to make small talk. He knew he should be paying closer attention to what the man was saying, especially as somewhere in all the bragging, there were details pertinent to this quarters profits for the boutique hotels the man owned.

He knew Liam was seriously considering acquiring the smaller chain. The idea was fiscally sound, he supposed, but he didn't like the strings that came with the arrangement. Gene made it clear on numerous occasions that he was open to a sale, but he wanted to keep the chain 'in the family'.

He could feel his hackles rising as Liam hugged Caroline. His brother walked her to the valet, something he never did for any of their other business associates.

Once upon a time, Trick would have bet anything his brother would never do anything to jeopardize his precious bachelorhood, not even for the sake of business. Now, he wasn't so sure.

If he marries the ice queen to guarantee the sale, I will personally kick his ass all over the dojo.

Gene reached out to shake his hand with his sweaty paw, pulling Trick out of his distraction in time to see Tahlia crossing the lobby floor. She was coming from the direction of the security office, where she had no doubt been visiting Peyton. Those two were inseparable lately.

"Goodbye, Gene," he said, giving the man a tiny push in the direction of the waiting car. "I'll be sure to give your suggestions to the concierge service some thought," he promised, lying through his teeth.

"See that you do! I'm telling you, it's a must for the high flyers," Gene said, clapping him on the back with all his might.

Trick suppressed a wince and smiled unconvincingly. *I swear he does that because I'm taller than him.* Gene was only about five-foot-five, shorter than his Nordic goddess daughter. He'd always been insecure about his height.

Once Gene cleared the doors, Trick hurried after Tahlia. His long legs ate up the marble tiled floors in record time. If they'd waxed them recently, he might have broken something. He nodded to Juan and Andre, the two security guards manning the front entrance. An additional two men were stationed discreetly at the back.

His sister Maggie worried aloud that the obvious uptick in the amount of security would turn off their elite clientele, but it had the opposite effect. The dark-suited men resembled secret service agents with their earpieces. Their guests assumed a high-ranking politician or celebrity was staying at the hotel. It increased the hotel's bookings.

He blocked the penthouse elevator door with his arm before it closed. Tahlia didn't even look up.

"Hey, Ace."

Her blue eyes blinked a few times before focusing on him. "Hi. I thought you were in a meeting until five."

"It's six o'clock."

"*Oh.* I guess I lost track of time. I've been teaching Peyton how to play poker, up until she had to leave for class. She's pretty good."

"She would be." He smirked. "I'd have taught her long ago if she'd asked. But she was always busy with Maggie or school. She's close to getting her degree in computer science, too. Not that she needs it."

The pensive tension around her chin relaxed. "Yes, she told me. Although, I'm wondering why she is doing it all at a no-name night school. She's smart and driven. She'd do well in at Harvard or MIT."

"I agree, but up until recently, her finances had a massive drain in the form of her butthead father. It's a long story, one I'm sure she'll tell you soon enough. You two have grown very close..."

"She's fun. Between her and Maia—it's like having real friends."

"They are your real friends."

She blushed. "I—yes. Yes, they are." The bright happy expression didn't last. She lapsed into silence, staring off into the distance.

"Are you okay?"

Her head jerked up. "I hope so."

He frowned as the elevator dinged, opening on the penthouse floor. "What's going on?"

It had been weeks since the warrant was issued for Tahlia's arrest, but they were using every legal resource at their disposal to get it rescinded.

Their lawyers were cautiously optimistic. The Boston police department declined to serve the warrant until some of the discrepancies in the case were resolved. Thanks to Ethan, the flight plan listing Tahlia as a passenger helped invalidate the timeline her family was trying to establish. But he was still working on getting actual crime-scene photos.

"Ethan called. He heard from the cops in Florida. They've decided to cancel the warrant."

"Well, that's great news!" Why was she upset? This was cause to celebrate.

Tahlia rubbed her arms, stopping outside of her suite door. "It's good news."

"But?"

"But you don't know my family. This won't be the end of it. I'm just waiting for the other shoe to drop."

She began to open the door to the suite when he stopped her. "Tahlia, no matter what they throw at us, we'll handle it."

He paused, his hand on the door. As sumptuous as the suite on the other side was, it didn't make up for not being able to go outside. "I know it doesn't help you've been stuck in the hotel this entire time."

They tried to make up for that. Maia and some of Tahlia's classmates from the math department came for dinner once a week. They joined his siblings for meals every other night. Tahlia was also hard at work revising her dissertation, so she kept busy.

She cuddled against him before going inside. Her hands swept up to encompass the room. "As prisons go, this place is freaking awesome. I'm lucky. There are some nice people working here. Some hot ones, too."

She moved her hand to cup his ass cheek.

Trick didn't need any more encouragement. He had her naked and underneath him in her bed less than a minute later.

Guilt flared as he noticed the fingerprint-shaped bruises on Tahlia's hips and thighs. *Crap.*

Ever since he'd learned the details of her father's death, he'd gone off the deep end. But he couldn't seem to help himself. A relentless hunger overwhelmed him every time he touched her.

And I used to think I was so civilized. Now I'm little more than an animal.

Trick knew he had to calm the fuck down. He was leaving

marks on her for the love of God. But this resolve flew out the window whenever he lay his hands on her.

Thankfully, Tahlia was stronger and putting on weight. She was no longer the gaunt figure she'd been when she first her arrived. Her golden curves were fuller, the creamy glowing skin an unholy temptation.

"*Patrick.*" Tahlia gasped as he flipped her over, pulling her onto her hands and knees. He slipped on protection, taking hold of his cock and rubbing it between her creamy cheeks before working the rigid staff into her tight sheath.

Undulating like a siren, she rocked back, swallowing his length up, enveloping him in her sublime heat. "Fuck, you feel so damn good."

This was better than drinking. It was better than any drug he'd tried. Hell, it was better than winning at poker.

That's good. Cause once you marry her, you'll never win a game again.

That didn't matter. He'd willingly lose every hand if it meant having this for the rest of his life.

Trick let his head fall back, languorously pumping in and out, letting his rhythm build slowly and then fast until his hips were slapping against her satin and gold backside. The feel of her was everything.

The only thing that would have made it better would be to take off the condom, to feel her naked heat wrapped around him. He'd only skipped protection the one time. As much as he knew he wanted to marry and have a family with Tahlia, they didn't have to start right away. She deserved to see the world and have some fun before that—as soon as he got rid of the threat hanging over them.

Sweet Jesus. Tahlia was moaning now—literally his favorite sound in the world.

Trick hissed involuntarily when she flexed her inner muscles, clenching around him, threatening to strangle his length. He tried to count hotel staff in his mind, anything to last a little longer, but Tahlia wasn't helping.

The curve of her ass, the line of her thighs as she strained against him—not to mention that long sweep of golden skin of her back. He'd never seen anything sexier.

Her long brown hair was too much of a temptation. Trick nudged her down until she was lying flat. He licked the back of her neck, wanting her taste in his mouth. He took hold of the length of her hair, wrapping it around his fist as he pounded, fucking her until he went blind.

Unable to hold out any longer, he let go, erupting with a convulsive wrench. Tahlia unsuccessfully buried a scream in the mattress, shaking and shivering as she climaxed with him.

When his awareness returned, his face was buried in Tahlia's hair. It smelled like vanilla. There was also some in his mouth.

He removed the strands with his index finger before shifting to trace the line of her hips with his fingers. A faint white web of tiny stretchmarks marked them but they only enhanced her beauty, saving her from being utterly perfect.

"This may be the wrong time to ask this, but I was wondering if you wanted to move into my suite."

"What?"

Tahlia's voice was hoarse, as if her throat hurt from screaming.

It's a good thing the walls are pretty soundproof.

He was still having a hard time speaking, too, but he needed to get this out. "It's more of a symbolic move. You can still use this suite as an office. But perhaps, you could move your clothes. We spend every night together anyway. I want to make it official."

Tahlia twisted to meet his eyes. "Are you sure you don't mind? It may be symbolic, but you'd still be giving up your space."

He couldn't bring himself to pull out of her, and she was wondering if he minded living together?

He kissed her. "Waking up with you every morning is my current plan for the next fifty or so years."

She wiggled out of his arms, but only to turn around to face him in order to press her gorgeous lips to his.

"Yes," she whispered. "I'll move in with you."

"I hope you don't mind, giving up what little space I've been giving you."

Her mouth quirked, but her eyes began to shine suspiciously. "I've been alone all my life. I don't need space."

Trick rolled over, pinning her back to the bed. "Good. Cause you're not getting any, not any time soon."

CHAPTER 23

Tahlia hurried down to the Parisian-style café on the ground floor. It was one of her favorite places in the hotel. From the intricate art-nouveau lithographs gracing the walls to the brass accents on the coffee bar, it personified the Paris of her imagination, a spot she hoped to experience in person someday.

In the meantime, she drank strong coffee and ate chocolate and almond croissants pretending, quite easily, that she was in France without ever leaving the safety of the hotel.

Patrick told her only the decor was French. In truth, the layout of the cafe had been modeled after a little place he liked in Morocco. That didn't matter to her. Regardless of the true inspiration, it was beautiful.

She was more excited than usual to get down there today. The front desk had called and told her Gina was waiting there to see her. It was a surprise visit, but a welcome one.

Gina was probably in town to scout out schools with her daughter. She'd mentioned her daughter Jenny's interest in a few Boston-area colleges several times and talked about visiting Tufts and Brandeis the last time they spoke. It was part of a mini-college tour she was planning.

I guess business finally calmed down enough for Gina to get away. Perhaps getting on the Caislean's preferred vendor list finally convinced her she could afford it.

Patrick was in meetings all day again, but hopefully, she could catch him in between two of them so she could introduce him to her friend. She knew Gina would be thrilled to meet one of the hotel's owners—and it would be a lot less intimidating for her if that someone was Patrick and not Liam. Maggie was still away, covering for Patrick at some of their European properties, but the third-party vendors weren't her purview in any case.

Tahlia walked into the cafe with a spring in her step, excited to catch up. She knew as soon as she saw the expression on Gina's face that something was terribly wrong.

Her first instinct was to turn and search for threats, but there was nobody there outside of the Caislean's friendly and efficient staff. Holding her breath, she walked over to Gina and sat down, her eyes darting around before settling on her friend.

Gina watched her with stark dry eyes—too wide. "You're not wrong. They've been to see me."

Tahlia's heart sank. Gina stared down at the table, her fingers tracing aimlessly over the fine honey pine surface.

"They threatened you, didn't they?"

"No." Gina's mouth twisted. "That wouldn't have worked."

Tears stung her eyes. "Then it was Jenny they went after."

She knew how Uncle Lucas thought. He was ruthless when it came to getting what he wanted.

Tahlia started to rise, her impulse to run to Patrick, or to get Ethan and Jason down here, but Gina waved her back down.

"Don't worry. Jenny is fine. Her father is watching her at home."

Gina's ex was a former junkie who hadn't managed to clean up his act in time to save his marriage. Tahlia had never met him, but she knew his reputation was that of a hard man, one Gina would rather not deal with unless necessary. The fact she'd contacted him to watch her daughter was enough to convince Tahlia she knew the threat was real.

Don't cry. The whole hotel would know something was wrong if she did.

"What did they want you to do?"

Gina pulled an envelope from her bag. Tahlia took it from her hands with trembling fingers.

Stop it. Falling apart wouldn't help anyone.

Her fingers were so numb she could barely open the envelope. Tahlia peeked inside, her heart pounding, expecting a note detailing the dire consequences of not returning home to Florida. But it wasn't a note. It was a picture.

"That's your young man, isn't it?" Gina asked as Tahlia stared at the photograph, the blood draining from her face.

Too overcome to speak, she nodded.

It had been taken from the street just across from the hotel. Patrick was standing next to a car in from of the hotel, chatting with one of the valets, presumably while he waited for his car to be brought around.

Tahlia traced his handsome face. It was open and friendly, the same expression he wore every day as he dealt with a staff he considered more like family.

A huge red slash was drawn through his neck. Tahlia crumpled the picture, holding it against her stomach. Words wouldn't have been as effective.

"I'll go back to them."

"No."

Gina shook her head until her greying ginger curls flew. "Don't you dare. Not for me and not for him."

"I can't stay here anymore."

They knew about Patrick now. They must know everything to have made a specific threat against him. He wouldn't be safe until she gave herself up.

Gina hmphed, taking her hand in a tight grip. "I don't know what these people want with you, but it's evil. They're evil."

She snatched the balled-up photograph from Tahlia's unresisting hands. "You need to *run*. Get yourself out of here. Go someplace safe and regroup."

The older woman held up a hand. "I know what you're thinking. You ran scared the last time. This time, run *angry*."

Gina exhaled harshly, her eyes sweeping Tahlia up and down. "I know it seems weird coming from me, the messenger. But those assholes made me mad, and that's what you need to be. You're stronger than you think. According to your boyfriend, you have a one-of-a-kind mind and crazy mad skills. Use them. Come up with a plan. And then you get them."

She pulled back, her face almost as red as her hair. "This isn't over yet. Use those brains. Think of a way to make them sorry. Make them hurt. I know you can. *Do it*."

CHAPTER 24

Trick was shaking with anger. "What do you mean *she's gone*? We have cameras everywhere. How could no one have seen them take her?"

No one had seen Tahlia in over twelve hours. He'd gone to meet her for lunch in their room when he first noticed she was gone. At first, he assumed she'd lost track of time with Peyton, or had holed up somewhere to work on her nearly finished dissertation.

When he didn't find her, he assumed she was at the pool, which was part of her routine now that she had left the cane behind. He texted, reminding her to meet him for dinner. But when she didn't turn up for that meal, he started hunting her down.

The entire hotel had been searched. None of the guards posted at the doors or the camera's trained on them caught her, which relaxed him for a minute.

She's probably fallen asleep somewhere. Maybe she'd gone for a massage and passed out in one of the spa suites. He called the staff there to ask.

The spa employees hadn't seen her all day. Trick was fighting off a panic attack in the security center, going through the feeds with a worried Peyton when Liam walked in.

Trick glanced up, but he ignored his brother's grim expression. He always looked like that these days. "Can you check the south doors again? Maybe someone came in that way."

Peyton shook her head. "I've checked there. I'm telling you after that Gina woman left, Tahlia went back to your suite. Has she called you back yet?"

"N—"

"*Patrick*."

He turned to his brother. "What?"

"Her things are gone."

Trick blinked. "What?"

"I was just in your room. I wanted to see if she'd left her phone in the bedroom. It was still plugged into the wall."

"I know, I saw that when I went upstairs."

His brother's face could have been carved from stone. "But you didn't check the closet."

Trick's chest tightened. "No, I didn't. Why?"

"Her clothes are gone. So is one of your travel suitcases."

He stared at his brother. A buzzing sound started in his ears, and it was getting louder. "She wouldn't leave me. She knows this is the only safe place for her."

"Not anymore." Liam handed him a mangled piece of photo paper—a photo of him.

The huge red slash through his body told him everything he needed to know.

"She left to protect me."

"AND YOU'RE sure she didn't go to Florida?" Ethan asked for the tenth time, opening a beer and setting it down untouched.

"Because we haven't heard a peep from those assholes. Maybe it's because they have what they wanted."

Trick rubbed his hands over his face, exhausted. He could always count on Ethan to be the voice of doom.

If only he and Liam would stop snipping for more than an hour at a time. They were so similar and would undoubtedly be great friends… if they didn't hate each other so much.

"Not according to Gina." He sighed heavily. Tahlia's ballsy friend had been more subdued the last time he talked to her. "She told Tahlia to run and regroup."

He'd been sick to his stomach when he'd heard about the threat to the woman's daughter, enough he hadn't railed at her for what she'd done.

If only she'd come to him before seeing Tahlia. He could have convinced her they could protect Jenny.

At least she told Tahlia to run and not give herself to those bastards. He could only pray Tahlia heeded her advice.

She'd been gone for over a week. As Liam had discovered, she'd taken most of her new clothes, her fake ID, and all the Visa gift cards he'd given her to buy whatever she wanted from the shops downstairs.

She'd refused to use the cards when he first gave them to her, but he'd insisted they sit in her drawer unused in the hopes she'd change her mind. The grand total for all the cards combined was in the ballpark of a few grand.

At least she has some cash. The question was where would she take it?

"I still don't get how she got past your security unless she had help," Ethan grumbled, giving him the side-eye.

"Peyton didn't help her. She knew how much was at stake."

"And just where is Peyton?" Ethan glanced around as if looking for her, then glowered when she didn't magically appear.

He did that quite a bit when he was visiting the hotel.

If only Peyton could see something in Ethan and not my idiot brother. Her life would be so much easier.

"Sleeping. She's been scouring the poker boards for me. She's was up all night setting up some tracing programs. She's trying to track Tahlia's alias."

Peyton was also monitoring the dark web at his behest, but he knew better than to mention that aloud to the FBI agent. She was trying to dig up anything she could find on Tahlia's family and their dirty deeds.

A flash of guilt passed over him as he saw Ethan pick up another file. His friend had devoted a lot of hours to this, and he deserved to know everything they were up to. But sometimes the lines they had to cross for the sake of expediency didn't mesh with Ethan's narrow point of view. Black or white. That was how the agent's mind worked.

If Peyton turns up anything, I'll tell him, of course. But until then, what Ethan didn't know wouldn't hurt him.

"If she's smart—and despite going for you, I think she is—Tahlia dumped that ID and got a new one." He picked up another paper, the entry logs for the passcode-protected doors.

"Well, there's an unauthorized exit from the laundry around an hour after Gina visited. It might be nothing. There's a lot of those."

Trick leaned back in his office chair. "It's where the hotel's smokers go to get their fix. We are more concerned with unauthorized entrances back there."

Employees needed to scan their keycards to get back in.

Ethan picked up the beer and took a sip. His eyes were narrowed on the security guard logs. "If this was her, then Tahlia picked the only time when the hallway to that entrance was not monitored. Just our luck."

Trick's cheek twitched. There was that damn word again. He'd lost count of the number of times someone had brought up luck or described Tahlia as lucky in the past few months. Given the circumstances, it irked him to no end.

"If she's not hiding here in Boston, and she's not in Florida, then where would she have gone? Back to New York?"

Mulling, he picked up the letter opener—the one Tahlia had fiddled with on his desk. "It's possible. She's not well-traveled and doesn't know any other cities well."

"What about Atlantic City or Las Vegas? She'd want to earn some money, right?"

"I thought of that. I have men checking the casinos out, but if we assume her family is aware of her gambling, then that doesn't feel right." It was still a possibility, of course, which was why he was circulating Tahlia's description to all his contacts there and in Reno again. But it was also too obvious.

"Can you gamble at any of those places?"

Trick gave himself a little shake. Ethan was watching him expectantly. "What places?"

Ethan rolled his eyes and pointed over Trick's head. He spun the chair to face the line of photos, all the hotels in the Caislean chain.

Caught with the idea, he stood to examine them more closely. "None have an in-house casino, but you can gamble in quite a few of these cities."

He trailed off as he turned back to Ethan, his eyes landing on the framed photograph of himself playing in Monaco on his birthday.

Would she? "I certainly would," he murmured aloud.

"What the hell are you going on about now?" Ethan scowled.

He let out an admiring huff. *Trust the woman you fell in love with. She knows what she's doing.*

"I don't suppose you have any more vacation days coming your way?"

Ethan snorted. "You and your family have sucked all those away for the next ten years."

He picked up the picture. "Too bad, because you'd love this place. If my hunch is correct, I'm going to find Tahlia safe and sound. I won't need backup."

He tossed the frame into Ethan's lap before going to notify their on-call pilot. The man needed to fuel up the Caislean jet ASAP.

TRICK HELD HIS BREATH, leaning back as he watched the most beautiful woman in the world cross the casino floor.

The Casino Monte Carlo, better known to James Bond fan's as the Casino Royale, was packed with well-heeled patrons, but none of the other ladies in the room even came close to Tahlia.

She walked with her head held high, as regal as any queen.

And damn if she didn't look the part. She was wearing a gorgeous red dress, a floor-length number that flowed behind her with a tiny train, almost like a wedding dress. But this was nothing like the virginal white gowns he saw in magazines. Though modestly cut at the bodice, the gown had a long slit up the side that made him want to punch every man who looked at her—and those were numerous. It felt as if every male's eye was on her.

Fuck, I don't blame them.

The dress glowed like a ruby against the gilt and dark wood interior. Opulence and luxury was the byword for this place. And yet, there was no jewel that shone more brightly than her.

Were those bodyguards hers? Two men in dark suits were stationed nearby keeping a careful distance. Tahlia acknowledged one with a nod before she settled at a table. The man nodded back, but in a curt professional way. They had the bearing of hired security.

Trick sipped his whiskey, opting to keep his seat near the bar so he could watch Tahlia play from a safe distance.

By rights, he should have been angry. He'd been through hell since she left with only the crumpled photo as a note. But at this moment, all he could feel was pride.

When Tahlia ran the first time, she'd ended up on the streets. But his girl was a fast learner. No more skulking at the fringes for her. She was hiding in plain sight here in his own personal Mecca, living the life that should have been hers to begin with.

But not without me. Trick would fight whoever he had to stay at her side. At the moment, that included Tahlia herself.

What did that make him?

He snorted to himself. *I'm a royal consort—the kid who has to run the gauntlet before he can win his place at the queen's side.*

Trick waved over Felix, the hotel's majordomo. "I need a favor. And before you say no, don't forget who introduced you to your girlfriend…"

CHAPTER 25

Tahlia walked down the hall of the Hotel de Paris flanked by her new bodyguards. She'd won thousands of dollars tonight, but it felt like a hollow victory.

Focus. Her plan was working. With tonight's earnings, she was nearly halfway to the first benchmark she'd set for herself. She was going to win a quarter of a million dollars.

Tahlia left everything when she'd left Boston—her new friends and Patrick. She missed him so much she could hardly sleep each night. The bed in her sumptuous hotel suite felt so empty.

Getting close to him had been stupid. Not only did she put him in danger, but unless she found a way to fight her family, she was going to have to live with this broken heart forever.

I will do it. I have to. That was why she'd come to Monaco. If there was any place for a gambler to regroup, it was here.

Her room in the Hotel de Paris was nowhere near the size of her suite at the Caislean, which was clean, open, and modern. By comparison, this hotel was old-fashioned, with its crystal chandeliers and heavy dark furnishings. All the gold and gilt accents should have been dated or cheesy, but they weren't. It was magnificent.

I should be excited. Monte Carlo was literally something out of her dreams, but without Patrick, she couldn't enjoy it.

At least I fit in. Tahlia had been careful on that score. Always a great mimic, she donned the disguise of a socialite with money to burn. It had been a bluff. Her fake ID, a top-notch Canadian passport, had been very expensive. When she arrived in Monaco, she had enough money left to cover her room and a few hands at the tables. But her luck held. After a few nights, she made enough money to upgrade to a suite in a bigger hotel and to buy a few essential items—this satin dress and her two new best friends.

Tahlia had debated hiring the bodyguards. She wanted to feel secure, but worried about the trustworthiness of strangers. If their protection was for sale, her family could afford to bribe them to give her up. In the end, she gambled on the anonymity given by her new identity and the vibe of decency she felt from the men in question, both former military personnel.

Alfonse, one of her bodyguards, paused on the oriental carpet runner in front of the doors to her room while Nolan took her keycard to open her door. Checking her room before she retired for the night was part of their routine.

Holding her purse in front of her, she mentally reviewed her winning and losing hands while Nolan did his check.

"*Hey,*" a man shouted.

Tahlia's head snapped up. Alfonse pushed her against the wall. "Wait here."

He ran inside to help Nolan. More crashing. It sounded as if something heavy hit the floor before another muffled male voice cried out her name.

Fear flooded through her as she peeked through the door. Was it one of her cousins or did they hire another goon to come get her?

She gasped, recognizing the brown hair trapped in a headlock under Nolan's arm.

"*Patrick*!" Tahlia ran inside. "Oh, God. Let him go."

Nolan obediently released him, letting a red-faced Patrick slide to the floor. He sat there with his eyes watering, coughing and reaching up to her. Tahlia got on her knees, wrapping her arms around him.

"I...I wanted...to surprise you," Patrick wheezed. He coughed, holding his hands to his throat.

Her bodyguards glanced at each other. Nolan shrugged.

"Do you require medical assistance?" Alfonse asked in his thickly accented English.

Patrick continued to struggle for breath and shook his head.

"Are you sure?" She frowned, holding his shoulders tight.

He waved away her concern. "I'm fine."

"Who is this?" Nolan asked her, his lips turned down.

"I'm her fiancé, Patrick Tyler."

Tahlia's mouth dropped open. Patrick could barely speak, but he managed to wreck her composure and stake his claim with one sentence.

Nolan's thick eyebrows rose. "Is that true?" His tone was tinged with disbelief. She could see the wheels turning in his head.

"Close enough." Tahlia's smile was a little forced. "Don't worry, he's not the reason I hired you. If you don't mind leaving now, I'll see you tomorrow morning."

"Not too early," Patrick interjected, getting to his feet with a sour scowl at Nolan.

A corner of Nolan's mouth turned up in the tiniest smirk, but he nodded at her. She walked him and Alfonse to the door, closing it so they could hear the door latch securely behind them—also part of their routine.

She stayed there, trying to gather her defenses.

"*Tahlia*."

That tone did nothing to calm her racing heart.

Pivoting on her heel, she turned to face him. Her lover's face was unreadable.

"Are you angry with me?" she whispered.

Didn't he know why she had to leave? She never meant to hurt him. Hell, she was trying to *save* him.

Patrick watched her, his expression hardening. Then he opened his arms. "That depends on how fast you can get out of that dress."

Tears sprang to her eyes as she stumbled toward him. He embraced her, engulfing her in his heat.

They were miles from Boston, but it felt like home.

His lips pressed to her forehead. "I'm sorry. That was terrible. I should have rehearsed a better opening line."

"That's not why I'm crying." She sniffed. "Patrick, you can't be here. You have to stay away from me. My family—"

He squeezed her tight. "I know all about their threats. I spoke to Gina, and we found the picture in your desk."

"Then why are you here?" Didn't he understand? If anything happened to him, she would never forgive herself.

Patrick stroked her cheek, wiping her tears away. "How can you even ask that? We belong together and nothing—not even your crazy insane family—is going to scare me away."

"But—"

"Shh." Patrick pressed his lips to her, silencing the rest of her protest. "First the dress. Then bed…and tomorrow, we start again."

Tahlia stopped crying, holding on for dear life as Patrick unzipped her gown. He pushed the sleeves off her shoulders with a long caress, letting it drop to the carpet in a shimmering cascade of red satin. His suit hit the floor next to it a few seconds later.

Patrick buried his hands in her hair, pulling her closer until she was pressed against him.

"I love you," he whispered.

Her heart felt like it was going to beat right out of her chest. "I love you, too." Her vision blurred, making the hard planes of his face waver.

The room swam, and she landed on the mattress with a gasp. Cool air chilled her body as he leaned away. He ran his hands over the black lace bra, slipping his fingers underneath to cup her breast.

Tahlia arched, her body growing wet as Patrick's heat burned her sensitive skin. He brushed her nipples roughly, making them peak as if begging for more of his touch. The bra melted away. Her panties quickly followed.

His hard length pressed against her, running over her heated softness with delicious friction.

Patrick pulled away, reaching for his pants. Tahlia sat up, covering his hand when he pulled out a condom.

"It's okay." After a visit from Eric, the hotel's concierge doctor, a month ago, she'd started the pill. Despite the fact she hadn't expected to see Patrick for a long time, she'd brought them along, taking them in an act of almost defiant hopefulness.

Unaware of her preparations, Patrick frowned. "Are you sure?"

She answered with an open-mouthed kiss, taking his length in her hand and guiding him to her entrance, telling him about her preparations in a whispered confession.

His demeanor changed, transforming into primal hunger she could feel. His feral satisfaction beat on her as he pressed, driving inside her with a groan.

Mouth gaping, Tahlia parted her legs wider, pushing down on the mattress with her heels to meet him halfway.

She would never get used to this—that moment when his hard cock took possession would always destroy her. Equal parts pain and pleasure, she could only hold on and surrender, giving herself over to that voracious fire that started whenever they were together like this.

Little sparks lit behind her eyes as he slid home. Tahlia panted as the head of his cock hit the entrance of her womb. "Oh, God, I love you. I love *this*."

"Fuck, me too," he gasped, his eyes squeezing shut.

He retreated and surged back, the hurried hungry slide of his cock splintering any last defenses she had. Tahlia lost herself, pulsing around him, trying to stroke him with her sheath until he cried out.

"Stop or I'll come too soon," he gritted out, pinning her hips and changing his angle so she couldn't move. He sped up, his hard thrusts rocking her entire body.

Her breasts shook with force, swinging in time to his bucking hips.

"No, not yet," she pleaded, scratching him involuntarily as she tried to fight the relentless crash of her orgasm. But it was too late. Her body crumbled, shivering as rapture claimed her.

Patrick held her quivering body close, his shaft still rock-hard inside her. "Don't worry, Ace. We're just getting started..."

CHAPTER 26

Tahlia woke shortly before noon, rough-skinned fingers stroking the sensitive underside of her breasts gently.

She'd slept like a rock, passing out after a few hours of frenzied lovemaking.

"I left bruises again. I'm sorry." Patrick's morning voice was as hoarse as she remembered.

She smiled, keeping her eyes closed. "I don't mind them," she mumbled.

Tahlia would rather feel this delicious soreness than let him be more gentle in bed.

Given her lack of experience, Patrick's forcefulness should have scared her. It had the opposite effect. There was an intoxicating quality to his touch, one that inspired a wild, unbridled response. She didn't want to give up that newfound freedom.

The little voice in her head told her she should be ashamed of herself. The things she let Patrick do to her were wrong—dirty. But she knew that wasn't *her* voice. It was the men in her family, their oppressive rules and restrictions that had no rhyme or reason. All of that crap burned away when she was with Patrick.

Was it possible for someone's first love to be their only one? *I think so.* She couldn't imagine this feeling existing with another man.

Patrick's fingers continued to work down until they reached the silky skin of her inner thighs. He pushed, parting her legs enough for his head to fit between. His tongue traced the seam of her lips, his teeth coming to graze her swollen clit.

Each flick of his tongue sent a pulse through her. Tahlia grabbed his head reflexively, her fingers clutching his silky dark hair.

The pressure inside her built with each stroke of his tongue. The explosion was coming, she could feel it starting when Trick suddenly rolled, flipping her with his strong hands.

"Ride me."

Startled, Tahlia blinked down at him. She was a bit high up along his chest for that. She began to move down, but he stopped her.

"I said ride me—my face. I want you to fuck my face." He nudged her, guiding until her pussy was hovering right over his mouth.

His hand reached up to cup her breast, the other holding her still with a grip on her ass cheek.

Embarrassment warred with confusion, but Patrick wasn't waiting for her to figure it out. He grabbed her, drawing her down until she was rubbing all over his mouth.

"Patrick." He had to be suffocating.

Tahlia tried to get off him, but he wouldn't cooperate. He plunged his tongue inside her, murmuring encouragement until Tahlia gave in, rocking above him as he ate her out.

It didn't take long for her to forget the awkwardness. His mouth was working its usual magic—driving all rational thought away and smashing through her inhibitions.

His teeth bit her clit a little harder and his tongue stabbed up, fucking her over and over until she pulsed, coming in his mouth with a ragged sigh.

Trick took a long last lick before flipping them. She landed on her back, his member thrusting inside before the spasms died away.

Tahlia's oversensitive body responded by immediately climaxing again. She bit Trick's shoulder, cutting off a scream as he pounded her into the mattress.

"That's it, baby. This time, come all over my cock."

The cords in his neck strained, and his self-control splintered. Tahlia clamped down greedily, riding the last pulses as he surged and jerked, spilling his hot seed in her tight sheath.

They collapsed in a sweaty tangle of limbs, her fingernails digging into his back. Patrick's steely arms slowly loosened their grip, his softening length sliding out, letting a cooling trickle leak out of her.

Soft kisses rained over her eyelids and lips. A few minutes later, Patrick went for a towel. She lay prone on the bed, still too weak to move as he lovingly cleaned her with a warm washcloth.

He's polishing me like I'm the silver. She giggled.

The bed dipped. His heat wrapped around her again. "Let's get married."

"What?"

Tahlia jerked, her eyes flying open just in time to get kissed in the eye. *"Ow."*

She clapped a hand over the smarting eye, tears streaming.

Patrick winced. "Sorry…but I'm serious. We should get married as soon as possible. Today if we can."

She coughed, suddenly having a hard time getting air into her lungs. Once she could talk again, she laughed. "You're insane."

He didn't laugh with her. His eyes burned like coals as one of his fingers traced her cheek.

"Tahlia, I know you don't have much basis for comparison, but this is not normal. What we have is special. More than special. It's a once-in-a-lifetime kind of love…and I don't want to lose it."

She could barely speak; her throat was thick with more trapped tears. "I—I don't want to lose it either. And I can see us spending the rest of our lives together, but…"

"We're not going to let your family get in our way. This is right."

Her lip quirked. "Will Liam and Maggie see it that way? Won't they kill you for getting married without them?"

"They'll get over it," he promised.

She sighed, guilt eating her alive. "I can't."

His eyes flashed. "Is it because of your family or is it me? Because if it's your family, fuck them. Those crazy assholes don't get to dictate your life. But if it's me you're not sure about, tell me now so I can change your mind."

She chuckled half-heartedly, even if it wasn't funny. Part of her wanted to lie, to tell him she didn't love him, but she couldn't bring herself to do it.

Tahlia had been born in a world full of secrets and lies. Nobody knew better than she did—there were some lies that couldn't be told. If they were, there was no going back, no way to make it right after.

She stared at his beautiful dark eyes. "I need to find a way to get my family to leave me alone first. Otherwise, I'll be a prisoner the rest of my life. And that will make you one, too. I don't want that for you."

He opened his mouth to speak, but she forestalled him by covering his mouth. "I'm not saying no. I want to find a way out from under this. That's why I came here. I had this half-baked idea I could make enough money to do something—fight back."

There was an adorable pucker between Patrick's dark brows. "Money I've got. It's all yours if you need it. What were you planning on?"

"Nothing solid. I…"

He ran his hand up her arm. "You can tell me anything. Maybe I can help."

She bit her upper lip. "I was thinking I should go on the offensive. But for that, I needed money. I made a bit so far, but I'm going to need a lot more."

He frowned. "Do you want to sue them?"

"Err…no. I want to frame them for murder and then blackmail them into leaving me alone."

His eyes widened. "I'm sorry, *what?*"

"I want to frame them for my father's murder."

"The one they actually committed?"

"Yes."

"Don't you think we should try and stick to legal courses of action? We just have to try to find evidence of the real crime."

Tahlia couldn't decide if that was naive or a sign of Patrick's inherent decency. She hated to sully that integrity with all her baggage.

"It won't exist. Trust me, I've been dealing with these people my entire life. They know how to cover their tracks. Even if my father's death was messy and unexpected, they have so much money, so much power, it would be impossible to find anything that could help us."

He leaned over, pressing a hard and unexpected kiss to her lips.

"What was that for?" she asked.

"For acknowledging it is *our* problem."

His lips compressed, a calculating expression darkening his eyes. "Do you think framing them could work?"

Tahlia shook her head. "Not really, but if you're contemplating my stupid plan, then you're as desperate as I am. No matter what dirty trick I came up with, my uncle Lucas would come up with something worse."

He rubbed her back. "We'll think of something. In the meantime, we shouldn't let your family get in the way of our future. In fact, getting married to me might make them think twice about coming after you."

"How conveniently you forget they threatened *you* this time."

"I can take care of myself. And not to brag, I'm connected to some powerful people. Never discount the advantages of influential friends."

He rolled over, letting the sheet slip off him. As usual, there wasn't a trace of shyness or discomfort over his nudity.

Why should he be ashamed? Patrick had a glorious body. He was tall and lean, fitter and more handsome than most models.

"For now, I think we should forget about your family. We're in one of my most favorite places in the world, and you have only scratched the surface of what it has to offer. Why don't we get dressed and go enjoy Monte Carlo?"

His bright enthusiasm chipped away at her misgivings and apprehension. "That sounds wonderful. Where do we start?"

He grinned. "With showers, but I'll take mine first."

"You don't want company?" This was new.

"I do. I really, *really* do. But you should call Maia and Peyton." He reached over and took his phone from his pants. "Do it from this. They're expecting your call."

Guilt swamped her. "Are they okay?"

He avoided her eyes. "Peyton's fine. Just a little worried."

Oh, no. "What about Maia?"

He handed her the phone. "She's back on bedrest."

"But she was off bedrest the last time I spoke to her!" Maia had even had lunch at the hotel a few days before Gina came to see her. Had Tahlia's action stressed her out so much she needed to be confined to her bed again?

"Stop that. It's not your fault," he said. "Maia's just tiny, and she's married to a *large* man. Calen towers over her. And since it's a boy this time, one that is obviously taking after his father, prolonged bedrest was inevitable. Don't worry. Calen has the best doctors watching over her."

Her breath caught. "It's a boy?"

He grinned and tapped the phone. "Call her now. She won't care about the time change." With that, he bounded off the bed, heading for the shower.

Tahlia spent the next hour groveling for forgiveness on the phone. Both Peyton and Maia were far too easy on her. They absolved her of any culpability for running out on them again. But she still felt awful when she was done.

It took Patrick less than an hour to put a smile back on her face. *And he managed to do it without sex*! she thought, beaming as he took her to the Terrasses de Fontvieille to view the royal car collection.

A racing enthusiast, Patrick went on and on about the Grand Prix, the famous formula-one race that wound through the narrow streets of the principality. Tahlia enjoyed the classic cars, but she was absolutely transported when he somehow finagled the keys to a vintage Porsche RSK Spyder.

"Don't worry. This isn't part of the normal collection," he assured her. "I rented this for a few days from a local dealer. You can drive it around to the end of the lot. After, I'll take over and we can do the whole Grand Prix circuit!"

"But Patrick, I don't even know how to drive a regular car," she confessed once the attendant who'd given him the keys was a safe distance.

"Shh," he whispered. "Just take it nice and easy. And step *lightly* on the gas."

He proceeded to give her more instructions, pointing out the clutch and pedals and explaining how different the race car handled from normal vehicles.

Jerking in fits and starts, Tahlia managed to drive the insanely rare vehicles a few dozen yards from where she'd started. She was relieved when they switched, and Patrick took the wheel. He zipped through the amazingly windy roads with natural ease. They went through the tunnel under the Fairmont Hotel and lapped the gorgeous harbor full of gleaming white boats.

For the next few days, Patrick showed her Monaco the way it was meant to be experienced. They walked the streets of Old Town, shopping and eating their way across the city. At night, Tahlia donned spectacular gowns. They wiled away the time gambling before retiring to her hotel suite to make love for hours.

Tahlia initially believed Patrick would want to dismiss the bodyguards she hired, but she was wrong.

"I think hiring them was smart," he said when she asked over breakfast a few days into his stay. "I took the liberty of making a few calls, and they're both solid professionals. I think they can be trusted."

"You checked them out?" She shouldn't have been surprised. Patrick wasn't the kind of man who left anything to chance.

He mumbled something, but his manner was a little evasive. "Is there something else?"

"You didn't tell them about your family."

Her throat was suddenly tight, which was unfortunate as she tried to swallow a large bite of omelet. She gulped juice to help it go down and cleared her throat. "But you did."

Patrick reached for her hand. "Tahlia, they needed to know. It's important they be aware of the nature of the threat to you. Based on what you told them, they assumed this was a routine job protecting a high roller when it's not." He leaned back in his chair. "Your bodyguards need all the information about the past attacks and the resources your family might throw at them.

She stared down at her half-finished plate. "I didn't think about it that way. God, they must hate me for putting them in danger. I should have known better than to drag more people into my mess. I have to apologize to them."

Patrick shook his head. "I'm not saying that. You did the right thing hiring them. And honestly, I think those guys can handle this. But forewarned is forearmed. They should be prepared. Not that anything is going to happen. Who in your family would expect you to be here of all places?" He gestured to the sumptuous suite around them.

Tahlia still felt terrible. "I should have told them. I just don't like talking about my family."

"I know, Ace."

She put her fork down, her appetite gone. "I was supposed to stay pure..."

He blinked at her. "What?"

"They kept boys and then men away from me. For the longest time, I thought I was going to be sold into the rich people's equivalent of white slavery—marriage to some rich old guy who would slap me around. I thought my virginity was a commodity to them. Now I think what they want is so much worse. And the kicker is if my brother hadn't died, my dad would have been okay with whatever it was... I don't think he even registered I was his child until both my brother and stepmother were gone, and he had no one else."

His smile was confused. "I know your whole world in Florida was messed up, but I have to believe your father was proud of you. I mean, you got your doctorate in math from Harvard for Pete's sake."

Her mouth twisted in a wry smile. "I don't have the Ph.D. yet."

"You do now. It came in the mail."

"It did?" Well, that was something.

"Yes. And one more thing—sex doesn't make you impure. There's nothing you can do that can change the goodness in your heart."

Tahlia tossed a strawberry at him. "Here's something to go with that cheese."

He tossed it right back, his aim infallible. It landed in her cleavage.

Patrick grinned, a wicked glint in his eye. He reached for her. "Here, let me help you with that."

They got a very late start that morning.

"WHERE DID YOU GET THIS?" Tahlia asked.

Patrick had surprised her with a trip to the harbor in the afternoon after they'd finally gotten out of bed. A sleek wooden speedboat gleamed in the bright sunlight. It looked like something that should be zipping along Venetian canals.

He shrugged. "I know a guy. I thought we could meander along the coast for an hour or so until the sun sets. Then we can go to this amazing little bistro a friend recommended for dinner."

He gestured to the two guards who'd accompanied them. "Alfonse spent some time in the navy, so he's going to drive while we split a bottle of this walnut wine and Armagnac aperitif I just discovered. Nolan's going to wait here and do whatever you do when there's only room for three in a boat."

"Sounds good." She giggled, letting him help her climb into the glossy cherry wood craft.

Sorry, she mouthed at the guards. She didn't know what was worse, being forced to watch her and Patrick be lovey-dovey or to get left behind entirely.

Nolan waved them off as Alfonse took the wheel with a surety that let her safely focus on Patrick.

He opened one of the wooden panels to reveal a miniature bar.

Tahlia stroked the fine leather of the seat. "This boat is incredible."

"If you want it, I'll buy it for you."

Tahlia scoffed as he handed her a small chilled glass of a brown liquid. "You can't buy me everything I like."

"Wanna bet?"

She shook her head at his irrepressible cheek.

He toasted her with the little aperitif glass. "Have you given any more thought to the future—aside from being married to me and having two or three of my babies…"

She choked and coughed, spitting out a little of the wine. "Can we just get married first?"

His eyes lit up. "So you accept?"

Frowning, she dabbed at the front of her dress with a napkin. "I thought I already had."

He cocked his head, a corner of his mouth lifting rakishly. "No, actually you didn't. Not yet."

A shiver passed through her, but it wasn't an unpleasant one. "Except for getting into school, I've never planned ahead for more than a week or two. Part of me was afraid to. I wasn't sure I was going to get a chance to have much a future, not one I got to decide myself."

He inhaled, gesturing to the harbor around them. "I've never been much of a planner either. I wouldn't have a hotel chain if not for my brother. He made the plans for world domination, and I would carry them out. I never gave my personal future much thought. Now it's all I can think about."

His gaze sharpened, the intensity threatening to singe her skin. "As for your family, what is it they say about getting back at someone? Living a good life is the best revenge."

Patrick pulled her close. "If your life is with me, I can promise something better than good. You deserve extraordinary."

Tahlia ducked her head, her cheeks hot. "Maybe planning ahead isn't such a bad idea."

His response was drowned out by a deafening boom.

CHAPTER 27

Trick hit the cold water of the Mediterranean with Tahlia in his arms. His brain registered the roar of the explosion a split second before his muscles reacted. He'd tightened his grip on the woman in his arms and bunched his thighs to launch them in the air. They'd gone over the side of the boat together.

Tahlia coughed, swallowing water and sputtering.

"Are you okay?" he yelled, letting go of Tahlia so she could tread water beside him.

She nodded her face milky white. The boat was a smoking pile in front of them. The entire engine block was burning—although the rear passenger area was still intact. *Shit.* How the hell had that happened?

His first thought was sabotage, the culprits Tahlia's family. But they were still alive. If this was an assignation attempt, it failed. The explosion hadn't completely obliterated the boat.

"Alfonse! Where's Alfonse?" Tahlia cried out, pumping her arms hard to keep her head above water.

"I don't know. Wait here." Trick pressed a hard kiss to her forehead before diving down under the wreck in search of the missing bodyguard. He surfaced on the other side, the salt water stinging his eyes.

The wide body of the bodyguard was floating on the other side of the burning speedboat.

Fuck!

Trick swam toward shore, his strokes strong and sure. He pulled on Alfonse's shoulders, relieved to see the man grimace.

Cloudy pain-filled eyes blinked at him.

"I think I dislocated my shoulder," Alfonse said, a trickle of blood running down from his hairline. Little red droplets sprinkled his face, which was peppered with shards of glass from the windshield.

Trick swore, yelling for Tahlia. She paddled around the boat and he panicked, immediately second-guessing himself. "No! Let's get as far from it as we can."

If this was sabotage, there might be a second explosion.

"We have to try to swim to shore."

Tahlia's face fell as she turned to the shore, rapidly calculating the distance. "I don't know if I can make it. I failed the Harvard swim test. I don't know how to swim real strokes."

Trick slung an arm under Alfonse, towing him along as he swam toward Tahlia. "It's going to be okay," he lied, wondering how the hell he was going to get them to the marina.

"Alfonse, can you manage on your own?" Maybe the man could float on his back, and Tahlia could hold on to him while he towed them back to shore.

Alfonse nodded, making a valiant effort to swim a one-armed sidestroke. He'd gone less than four feet before Trick changed his mind.

"Hold up," he said, positioning Tahlia so she was treading water closer to Alfonse. He spun round to face the boat. Was he fast enough?

I don't have a choice. He needed to get to the lifejackets.

He was kicking himself for not putting one on Tahlia to begin with, but he'd been too wrapped up in his plans for the perfect sunset cruise so he could ask for her hand in marriage again.

"Wait here. I'm going for the life jackets. We're going to need them."

He didn't wait for an answer, diving back into the water with a rapid freestyle. He reached the boat in seconds, climbing on the stern.

"Patrick, don't you dare get back on that burning boat!" Tahlia's voice was shrill with panic.

He didn't waste time answering. Instead, he threw up the cushion to reveal the storage spaces built into the seats in the back. The lifesavers were in the third one he checked. He grabbed two and jumped back into the water in one clean dive. He made it back to the others in less than a minute.

"Put this on," he ordered, anxiety making his voice curt.

Tahlia grabbed his arm with a death grip. "Don't you ever do that again," she sobbed.

"*I had to.* Now please, put this on!"

Tahlia hurried to obey, insisting on putting a jacket on Alfonse first. They could only manage to get the uninjured arm threaded through one armhole. The bodyguard managed to hug the jacket to his chest, helping him float. Once Tahlia put her jacket on, their battered trio began to paddle to the shore.

They beat at the water, limping along at a slow crawl for what felt like hours. Slowly, the land came closer and closer as the sun began to dip in the sky.

Damn, I don't want her out here in the dark. His thigh and calf muscles were burning, but he didn't give up. He needed to get Tahlia to safety.

The cold water began to sap his strength, but he ignored it. Then Tahlia's teeth began to chatter, and he swore aloud.

"Hang on, baby!" He started kicking harder, fighting to speed them up.

The arduous journey was cut short by a rescue a few minutes later. Nolan had spotted the smoke from the harbor and drafted a local with a small motorboat to come pick them up. Together, Nolan and the stranger managed to fish them out of the water. They were in the local hospital less than twenty minutes later.

Trick closely supervised the doctors as they treated Tahlia for possible shock, wrapping her in those foil blankets to keep her warm. He reluctantly left her under Nolan's care while he checked on the injured bodyguard. Alfonse got lucky, though. He was going to recover.

Interviews with the local police followed. The coast guard was able to recover the boat before it sank. They were taking it in to examine it for evidence of explosives.

Hours later, Nolan was finally able to drive them back to the hotel. Trick had an arm tightly wrapped around Tahlia. She was quiet, curled against his chest.

"We have to change rooms," Nolan said as he pulled up to the front entrance of the Hotel de Paris. "In fact, we should change hotels entirely."

He shook his head. "No. We're checking out. I'm having the Caislean jet meet us at the airport. I'm taking Tahlia back to Boston."

"What?" Tahlia's ice-blue eyes blinked at him.

"I know you were worried about bringing trouble home, but if this wasn't an accident, then we're better off back there."

"I don't th—"

He stopped her with a few fingers to her lips. "It won't be forever. I kept telling you to join a think tank as a job. After this, I realized we already have one. Between my family and friends and yours, we have the collective brain power of a small country. We're going to figure out what the hell to do next together. And while we're at it, we're going to get married because fuck your family. *Fuck* them."

"It could have been an accident," she protested half-heartedly.

He scowled at her, probably for the first time.

She held up a hand. "All right it wasn't. But what about Gina and Jenny? How do we keep everyone safe?"

Trick bent to kiss her forehead. "We'll figure it out."

They had to.

TAHLIA WATCHED the falling snow from the suite's living room window. The snowstorm had been going on for days, blanketing the city with a pristine white powder. At least that was how it appeared from a distance. Except for the roof garden, she hadn't set a foot out of doors since they returned a few weeks ago.

The traffic on the streets below was crawling at a snail's pace to avoid spinning out on the slushy streets.

Large swaths of Boston were on lockdown because of the weather. *Kind of like me.*

Staying indoors was part of the concierge doctor's advice. Their unintended dip in the Mediterranean in winter had given her a terrible cold, one so bad Patrick was convinced it was pneumonia. The illness had knocked her out for weeks. She was still a bit shaky and tired easily.

A ray of sunlight broke through the clouds, bathing her in warmth and light. It caught the massive stone on her left hand, making it sparkle and shine. Fingering the engagement ring, Tahlia closed her eyes, soaking up the bright rays before the clouds moved again.

She turned at the sound of the electronic door lock whirling open. A wave of dizziness came over her and she swayed, her vision momentarily darkening.

"*Hey.*" Tahlia glanced up to see Ethan rushing toward her. He cleared the couch in a jump and was at her side in a flash. He grabbed her arm, ushering her to the couch with a murmur.

"Are you all right?" he asked.

"I'm fine, thanks. It's just taking forever to shake this cold."

Ethan frowned but nodded anyway. He gestured to the kitchen area. "Can I fix you some tea? Or soup?"

She smiled weakly. "I ate with Maggie and Peyton a little earlier. Was there something you needed?"

At this point, Tahlia felt safe in calling the FBI agent a friend, but he wouldn't have come into the suite she shared with Patrick alone unless it was important. Ethan wasn't big on hanging out and chatting when he could be chasing down Peyton.

Ethan put his hands in his jean pockets. He pursed his lips. "I was looking for Trick..."

She tilted her head back in understanding. "But it's about me, or rather about my family, isn't it?"

"Uh...yeah." He shuffled on his feet. "We were wondering why things were so quiet since you and Trick got back from France, so I pumped a few contacts and they dug up a possible reason."

She leaned forward, her chest tight. "What is it?"

"Your uncle Lucas is being treated for cancer. He's been flying back and forth to Pennsylvania from the Florida estate. There's a pretty good cancer center at the university there."

Tahlia's lips parted. "I see."

What did this mean? Her family prided itself on their good fortune. No member had ever been diagnosed with cancer before.

"There's more."

She screwed her nose up, unsure if she wanted to know.

"Apparently, the whole family is up in arms about a series of financial reversals. It's nothing too major. They're not broke—unfortunately. Not yet. But all these little things cropping up should keep them busy for a while. My friend at the FCC thinks there's something fishy going on with them judging from their investment patterns. He's optimistic he can get something on them. In the meantime, my buddy Mason from Interpol is checking some of their overseas operations. Your family has a long reach, but we're going to find something on them. I don't want you to worry. Your family's bad luck is our good fortune."

Something about that last phrase made her skin crawl. "Yeah," she said, twisting her engagement ring absently.

"Don't tell Trick I said that by the way. He swears like a sailor anytime anyone uses that word."

"What word?"

"Luck. Or more specifically, he loses his shit when someone calls you lucky. But this is good news," he insisted.

That didn't make her feel any better, but she tried to appear more confident. "I know. Thank you."

Ethan grinned, his tone a little too deliberately upbeat. "That rock weighing you down? You should have Trick get you a normal-sized one that you don't have to drag behind you."

She lifted her hand into a fist. "It would make a good weapon, don't you think?"

"Yeah... So you said you had lunch with Peyton. She's in today?"

Tahlia nodded, her lip twitching. She'd had lunch with Peyton and Maggie, but Ethan had a one-track mind.

"Peyton should be at her desk downstairs. I actually forgot to give her something at lunch." She stood and went for one of the many boxes littering the dining room table.

She fished the wedding invitation with her friend's name on it out and handed it to Ethan. "If you're headed down there, can you do me a favor and give this to her? I'm not done addressing them all so the W's aren't done yet, but I can do yours really quick if you can wait."

Ethan tried not to beam at her. He snatched the invitation from her hand and was at the door before she could blink.

"Don't worry about it," he called behind her. "It's not like I don't know where it's going to be!"

He waved goodbye, rushing out without further delay.

She couldn't help but laugh. Ethan was shameless. She only prayed her friend would wake up and see what a great guy he was.

Tahlia remembered Peyton's face when she saw Liam with his girlfriend on the security feeds. Maybe that was too much to ask. Ethan had an uphill battle ahead of him. Things could get ugly.

However, there was nothing she could say or do that would help anyone involved. Resolving to not interfere, she went back to her wedding invitations before settling down in front of the computer for a little online poker.

A few hours later, her screen was filled with giant letters.

WINNER.

Tahlia gasped, watching the numbers in her pot jump an entire order of magnitude.

"Patrick!"

Damn it. He wasn't here. Tahlia rushed out the door to find him in his office, but he was out.

Oh, right. He was meeting with some vendors in the kitchens this afternoon. Tahlia hurried out, catching sight of Liam arguing with Peyton by the elevators.

She was too far to hear what they were saying, but it was obvious Liam was reading Peyton the riot act.

Concerned, Tahlia shuffled her feet, debating going forward to casually interrupt. Liam was a very private person. He'd probably stop picking on Peyton as soon as he saw she was there, witnessing it all.

Tahlia needn't have worried. Her friend was having none of it. The elevator doors opened behind them and Peyton stalked inside, flipping off Liam as she went.

Grumbling, he spun on his heel, checking himself mid-step when he saw her standing there.

"Hi," she said, wishing Peyton had waited for her.

"Hey." He waved the pile of papers he was holding. A dyed-in-the-wool workaholic, she'd never seen him without a document of some kind or another in his hands.

Liam passed a hand over his face before his head cocked to one side. His eyes narrowed.

"Can you talk some sense into her?" He pointed back at the elevator.

"To Peyton?" she asked, her eyes widening.

"Yes. She's insisted on staying at her dad's old place, but I want her to sleep at the hotel until this business with your family blows over."

"Uh..."

Their fight was her fault. She swallowed hard, gearing up for the long apology he was probably waiting for. "I am so sorry about that. I know you must wish me a thousand miles away. I'm putting everyone in danger and—"

He held up a hand cutting her off. "You have to stop with that. You're part of the family now... or will be soon enough. I just don't like Peyton staying on in that rattrap she calls home when there's plenty of room here. Especially now you've moved into Trick's rooms. The suite next door, the one you were in at first, is empty. She should sleep there. Do you think you can talk to her?"

"I can try," she hedged.

She didn't want anything to happen to Peyton because of her, but asking the other woman to come here to move down the hall from Liam sounded like a terrible idea.

He hesitated, the expression of doubt on his face unfamiliar. "Make sure she thinks it was your idea." He cleared his throat. "I'm not exactly her favorite person these days because of her deadbeat dad."

Tahlia nodded, a little surprised at the undercurrents she was detecting. Liam wasn't a demonstrative man, but she was too adept at hiding her own emotions not to know when someone else was doing it, too. Underneath, Liam was roiling.

Wow. She would have never guessed.

"I thought Peyton's father passed away."

"He died last year and good riddance. Unfortunately, his legacy of bullshit lives on," Liam growled.

Tahlia stared, unsure what to say. His face softened, and he thumped her on the back in what she guessed was supposed to be a reassuring manner.

"Donny is no loss, trust me. If he were still around, Trick wouldn't have let you near that asshole with a ten-foot pole."

"All right," she said, eyeing the elevator. The space between her shoulder blades stung a little. Liam was such a bear of a man, he must not know his own strength.

"Peyton likes the cheese danish from the cafe downstairs."

"What?" This conversation was getting away from her again.

Liam gestured with his papers. "You can butter her up with one before you bring up moving in here."

"Oh. Of course…" The elevators doors opened. *Freedom!*

She backed away. "I'm going to go do that now."

He waved her on. "Don't take no for an answer," he ordered.

The words were pretty much what she'd come to expect from Liam, but the expression in his eyes was something else.

Anger would have been expected. What she saw was…desperation.

CHAPTER 28

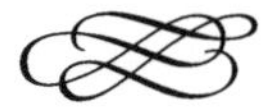

Tahlia was almost hopping up and down with excitement, dancing around the coffee table in their suite before hesitating. "Are you sure about this?" she asked, turning to her gorgeous fiancé.

"*Yes.*" Patrick was emphatic. "You don't need this money for our campaign against your family. If Mason is right, and he usually is, then Cain and Dante are guilty of a litany of white-collar crimes. It's a miracle they've managed to stay undetected until now."

Mention of her family dampened her enthusiasm. "It won't make that much of a difference if they don't get Uncle Lucas on something."

Patrick held up a hand. "We'll get him, too. If it's not Interpol, then the FCC will bring the hammer down. Trust me. But your gambling winnings won't make a difference."

She pressed the pamphlet Peyton helped her create to her chest. "Then I should put some of them toward our wedding expenses…"

"Liam won't take a dime from you, and you know it. And don't bother suggesting saving it for our children's college fund. That's done, too," he added with a wink.

She stood up straighter, holding the pamphlet with both hands. "All right then. I'm ready to do this."

'This' was a special education program run out of select women's shelters.

Despite her recent good fortune, Tahlia's experiences living at the fringes of society stayed with her. Patrick and his family were her inspiration. She admired everything the Tylers did to help women in trouble. She wanted to do her part, too.

To that end, she approached Maggie and Peyton for some help fleshing out an idea she'd first had while staying in a shelter in New York.

Tahlia was going to use her winnings to fund a vocational boot camp out of local shelters and hotels. In addition to providing beds for their guests and whatever children they had, the program was a crash course in math and computers. Participants would be trained in different vocational software. If they completed the course, they would receive a special certificate they could present to future employers. After the pilot program, she and Maia were going to work on getting the program official state certification.

If I can let go of my cash.

"I'm sorry I'm still hesitating. It's just that I get nervous. I've been seeing my winnings as sort of a shield against my family—even though I know it's nonsense. Money isn't going to stop them."

Trick pulled her close to his side. "We are going to put an end to all of this, but not with your poker winnings. There will be plenty more of that by the way, believe me. You're too good not to be a high roller."

He took the pamphlet from her hands. "Let's move on this now. You and Peyton are having so much fun designing the curriculum."

Tahlia let her head fall against his chest. "I feel guilty about that. I should be helping more with the wedding preparations."

He shook his head. "Only if you want. Maggie and I have that covered."

She pursed her lips. "Why don't you want me to help? Are you afraid I'll turn into a bridezilla or something?"

It wasn't the first time he'd declined her help.

"No, that's not it. I'm afraid you'll see all the wedding fripperies and get cold feet."

He showed his teeth in something that only loosely resembled a smile.

Tahlia nudged him with her hip, making him lose his balance. He landed on the couch. She climbed on his lap before he was able to recover. "I'm not going anywhere."

He gave her a mock exasperated look as if to say *finally* before bending his head to kiss her. Unfortunately, he cut their make-out session short a few minutes later with a groan.

"I hate to go, but I have a conference call." Patrick gently set her aside next to him. He stood, straightening his jacket and tie.

"Is it a video conference call?"

He nodded. "It's better if we can see the faces we're all making at each other," he joked. "Reading people's reactions helps with negotiations, but in this case, the Sydney group opted for it."

She hopped up, tweaking his tie. "Those Aussie surfer babes just want to check you out. I can't say I blame them. But you're officially off the market, mister."

A corner of his mouth turned up. "This conference is all men."

Waving that away, she sat back down with her pamphlet. "My comment stands. Go do your call. I should get my notes on this to Peyton. We're supposed to go over the second draft this afternoon."

He grinned and stole a long kiss before waving goodbye. No sooner did the door click behind him than she began to miss him.

I'm hopeless. But she was smiling when she thought it. And who could blame her for being preoccupied with her drop-dead gorgeous fiancé? Anyone who'd caught a glimpse of his ass in those fitted suit pants would be obsessed.

It is a perfect ass. Sublime and completely bite-able. Once or twice, she had taken a nip…

Back to work, she scolded herself. Grabbing a pen, she started jotting notes in the margins of her papers. Half the pages were covered when she finally remembered to check when Peyton was free.

A knock on the door interrupted her mid-text. Semi, one of the hotel's porters, was there with a delivery.

Accustomed to getting a slew of presents from Patrick, and now wedding gifts, she signed for the box and took it next to the dining table by the window to open.

The unmarked box held a phone with a wide new screen.

"He already got me a phone," she muttered.

True, it wasn't as fancy as this one, but Patrick needed to stop shopping online for her when he was working. He'd filled her closet with coats and expensive shoes. If he started with electronics, they'd be buried in gadgets.

The screen on the smartphone blinked on, making Tahlia drop it on the table.

She frowned. The impact must have turned on a movie. It appeared to be some sort of spy thriller. The phone displayed a live view of an office. There was a man was talking on the phone, his back to the screen. A red bull's eye was superimposed on his back. It shrank until the red laser sight was pointing at the man's head. Then he turned to face the window.

Patrick. It was Patrick. Someone was filming him from a neighboring skyscraper, and they had him in the sights of a gun.

Her half-strangled scream didn't make it past her throat. Tensing, she was about to run to Patrick's office when a voice stopped her. It was coming from the phone, playing over the silent video.

"Hello, Tahlia. My name is Killian. We are going to get through this together, but you have to listen to me. Do not move. Warning your boyfriend will only get him killed."

"What?" She couldn't think of anything else to say.

Shivering, she reached for the phone. A red laser beam bounced off the back of her hand. Gasping, she snatched it back.

"Why don't you sit down? We need to talk."

The voice on the phone was deep and smooth, more like the suave hero of a movie than the villain.

She didn't move.

"Tahlia. *Sit*."

Shaking from head to toe, she pulled out a chair and sat down.

"Good, now what I need you to do—"

"Hey, Tahlia! We got tired of waiting for you, so we came up."

Her head snapped up.

No! Peyton and Maggie had walked in holding three coffees in a cardboard holder.

Peyton was holding a danish. Tahlia didn't know why her mind seized on that.

The voice was not happy about the interruption. "*Tahlia*. Focus"

Maggie and Peyton blurred as tears filled her eyes. She snapped, rushing to her feet to wave at them frantically.

Get out, she mouthed.

Maggie frowned and stepped closer, but Peyton grabbed her arm, jerking her back. Her wide blue eyes were fixed on the bouncing laser light dancing all over Tahlia's limbs. Reacting, she tackled Maggie around the middle, pulling her down behind the long cream leather couch near the door.

"I don't like disruptions, Tahlia," the voice continued.

"It was the maids coming to clean. They're gone," she lied, hoping the man didn't have a clear view of the back of the room.

"Good. Now back to business. We need to get you out of there without interference. You'll have to go out the basement exit. It will be unmanned for a three-minute window at exactly seven forty-five. That's how long you have to get down there. There will be a car waiting for you. Take the phone."

Her hand shook as she picked it up. The screen zoomed in on Patrick again as if to remind her about what was at stake.

"I would wipe those tears," the voice said. "The entire staff watches you closely. You have to hold it together long enough to get out of the hotel. Make sure no one stops you."

Shuddering, Tahlia took one step toward the door. Then she took another, barely able to feel her own feet.

She scrubbed her face with her sleeve, holding the phone to her chest as she reached the couch.

Maggie and Peyton were huddled behind it. Peyton had her arms wrapped around Maggie's neck. The latter was sobbing, her hands pressed against her mouth to keep the noise trapped inside.

Peyton's eyes were wide and filled with fire. But Tahlia knew she wasn't angry at her.

"Don't go," she mouthed.

"I have to," Tahlia whispered back, her heart shattering into a billion pieces as she flipped the phone over to show them the screen.

Then she opened the door to the hallway, stepping out as the feed from the camera faded to black.

She didn't look back.

THE PENTHOUSE ELEVATOR was taking an eternity to arrive. Tahlia held the phone as if it were contaminated with the plague, but she couldn't afford to drop it. She knew the man was listening.

Perhaps he was bluffing. He could have some fancy laser pointed at Patrick, and not a gun.

You know it's real. And if there was room for doubt, she couldn't take the risk. Weak-kneed, she counted, willing the elevator to speed up.

Thankfully, it was empty. Stepping inside, she waited for more instruction, but the voice from the speaker was silent.

"Hold up."

Starting violently, Tahlia spun around. Liam stopped the elevators doors from closing. He joined her, his attention on the papers he was holding.

The carriage began to descend.

Tahlia kept her eyes on the floor, her body alternating from hot to cold and back again. She was praying Liam wouldn't notice her.

"What's wrong?"

Flinching, her eyes flew to him. Liam was frowning. She plastered a smile on her face. "Nothing."

The lines around his mouth deepened. She could see the suspicion growing in his eyes.

"Are you sure? You're pale."

She shook her head. "I'm fine."

His eyes narrowed. He crossed his arms and raised a thick dark eyebrow at her. "Then why are your eyes red?"

Damn it.

"Allergies?" She didn't mean to make it sound like a question.

His face softened. "Is it your family?"

Crap. Why did Liam have to be so perceptive all of a sudden? He was usually too wrapped up in work to pay her any mind.

"I talked to Peyton," she blurted.

Liam straightened and dropped his arms. "What did she say?" he asked, his dark eyes flaring.

Wow. She hadn't anticipated such an intense reaction. Liam was…eager. The man may not have been capable of returning Peyton's feelings, but she was important to him. Very important.

The image of the woman in question hiding behind the couch with a crying Maggie flashed through her mind.

"She's thinking about it," she hedged, fingering the phone. The voice was silent, but she knew he was there.

"In fact, I think Peyton wanted to talk to you about it some more. She said there were some ground rules you needed to agree to."

Liam smirked. "Of course she did."

"She wants to see you in her office. Trick, too, but I forgot to tell him that. Maybe you can pass that on for me?"

Peyton's office was on the ground floor—a windowless room filled with trained security officers.

The elevator opened, revealing the rear lobby area.

She hurried out, turning back at the corner. "I would go now while Peyton is still in a good mood."

Liam smiled at her—a heart-stopping grin that warmed his entire face. He resembled Patrick so much when he smiled it hurt to look at him.

"Thanks for convincing her for me. I appreciate it."

"No problem," she replied faintly, waving as he disappeared down the hall leading to the back offices.

"You're almost out of time," the voice reminded her once he was gone.

Tahlia flinched. She swallowed hard and headed for the basement stairs.

She didn't know how the voice learned so much about the hotel's internal security measures, but he had the guard's rotations down pat. He'd managed to find the one tiny moment when the men were changing shifts, leaving through the same basement door she used when she left for Monaco.

A wave of dizziness swept over her as she opened the door. There was a black sports car with tinted windows waiting in the alley.

"I am a lucky penny," she reminded herself.

Neck stiff from holding her head high, she climbed into the passenger seat.

CHAPTER 29

Trick hung up the phone with a satisfied smile. His surprise for Tahlia was starting to come together.

It took some wrangling, but he'd managed to get one of the Casino de Monte Carlo's old poker tables shipped here. It was going to be the centerpiece at their wedding reception. The entire event was going to be modeled after the casino Tahlia had fallen in love with.

Copies of the casino's over-the-top chandeliers were on their way. He was also having the event company send him red-patterned upholstery samples so he could pick chairs that fit the theme.

He reached for a pen to make a note when the door swung open. It swung so hard it banged into the wall. Maggie and Peyton burst inside, falling all over each other in the process.

"Get away from the window!"

THE HIRED assassin was incongruously handsome. He had thick dark hair and a straight Roman nose. His features weren't any one nationality or race, but a distinctive scar ran from the end of his right eye straight back to his hairline.

He was so calm, pulling away from the curb with a friendly little nod and a charming smile.

What the hell? At least the goon in New York had been a predictably evil-looking jerkwad. This guy acted like he was a long-lost friend.

Tahlia sat silently, her limbs weak with shock and panic. She couldn't seem to calm her racing heart. The man looked familiar. She realized he must have been staying at the hotel as a guest, so he could watch her.

She quickly lost track of their location. It was too difficult to scan for street signs when her entire body was trying to shut down.

"You should buckle up," he said solicitously.

Her head pulled back as she stared at him in disbelief. "Why? Aren't you driving me to the docks or some lonely warehouse district to put a bullet in the back of my head?"

He patted her shoulder. "No, of course not. You can let go of that phone by the way. You won't be needing it in Florida."

Tahlia buckled her seat belt with numb fingers. "So you're not going to shoot me? Because if that's an option, I'd rather you did."

The man laughed, a booming hearty sound. "My name is Killian. I mentioned it before, but I think you forgot."

"Sorry, the laser sight pointed at my future husband's head kind of wiped it from my mind. It's not every day an assassin comes after you. In my case, it's only every couple of weeks."

Killian flicked thick sooty lashes at her. "I'm not an assassin. At least not all the time. Funnily enough, the market for that sort is down, at least for the cases that fit my criteria. A man has to have standards. I'm very selective about my clients. "

"A selective assassin?" she asked flatly.

The cold surreality of her circumstances were pressing down on her. Nothing felt real—not the seat underneath her or the seat belt pressing against her chest.

Killian tsked, turning the wheel to pull onto the highway. "These days I call myself a facilitator. Your family wants you home by any means necessary. I make that happen with a minimum of fuss." He glanced at her. "Don't worry, your boyfriend is quite safe now."

The tight coil of anxiety in the pit of her stomach loosened a fraction. "Good," she mumbled, but then wondered why the hell she believed him.

The car sped along the road, weaving in and out of traffic with ease. "I did a little research on him by the way. Patrick Tyler is a pretty nice catch for a girl like you."

Her brows pulled together. "What the hell does that mean?"

The hired killer waggled his fingers without taking them off the wheel. "He's a young, attractive philanthropist. Excellent reputation, even among his ex-girlfriends. Very pro women's rights. And he's rich to boot."

Unbelievable. "I know what Patrick is. I meant the girl-like-you dig."

He frowned. "Do you honestly think that nice boy deserves a murderess for a wife—no matter how good she is at poker?"

Her mouth dropped open, the shock driving the numbness away. "A *murderess?*"

Killian sniffed a disdainful little sound.

"Who did I kill?"

He sighed, keeping his eyes on the road.

She buried her face in her hands. Her head hurt. "They told you I killed my father."

Her family had attempted to pin his death on her through legal channels. Why was she surprised to hear they would lie to an assassin as well?

Because killers for hire aren't supposed to have standards. Shooting people was just supposed to be a paycheck to professionals.

Except her family had fed Killian the patricide lie, which meant they at least believed in these fictional standards.

"The way I heard it, you couldn't wait for your inheritance," he offered. "That was when you decided to slip a little something in his afternoon coffee."

Tahlia groaned. This nightmare was swiftly turning into a farce. "I suppose my family told you they only want justice served, and they'll be turning me over to the authorities."

He shrugged. "If it makes any difference, I didn't buy that line. But there's something to be said about keeping things in the family. I've worked for a few outfits that worked that way."

"Let me guess...you were the one who fixed these internal problems for them?" she said, making air quotes around *fixed*.

"My reputation precedes me, I see."

Ugh. "I suppose you also believe I decapitated my father after I poisoned him?"

The car jerked a little as he twisted to look at her.

She could tell she'd surprised him. It was her turn to sniff. "I thought you did your research. Did you miss the part where my father's body was dismembered?"

Killian narrowed his eyes and stayed silent. Tahlia rubbed her forehead.

"Never mind," she muttered. "You and I both know your supposed standards are just some fake set of hoops you make your clients jump through to justify what you do. They're meaningless. You can stop pretending you care about a person's innocence. Just take the damn cash and murder indiscriminately because there's no difference to the people you kill."

The air almost vibrated. Tahlia knew she should have been

frightened by the touch of menace emanating from the hired killer, but she was past caring.

Whatever he did to her between now and Florida couldn't be any worse than what was in store for her there. She turned away, staring out the window as the city sped by.

The minutes stretched into an hour. Silence reigned as they pulled into a small airfield. A luxuriously appointed jet was waiting on a short runway.

She was going home.

TRICK AVOIDED HITTING a garbage truck by mere inches. He gripped the wheel and pulled into the narrow space between two SUVs before shooting across three lanes to enter the fast lane.

"Jesus, Patrick, you're going to kill us." Liam held onto the dashboard of the Mercedes by his fingernails.

He clenched his teeth, his eyes intent on the road.

"Update," he barked.

"We've eliminated Logan airport," Ethan said over speakerphone. He and Jason were following in their FBI-issued vehicle. Jason's line was connected to their office, where their fellow agents were scouring flight plans and pouring over traffic-cam footage.

"If it's not Logan, why the fuck am I on this highway?" His voice was both shrill and hoarse. Panic clawed at his throat.

"Breathe, damn it," Liam snapped from the passenger seat. He was clutching the doorframe now. "Crashing and killing us both won't help Tahlia."

"He has a point, Trick," Ethan said in a rare moment of solidarity with Liam. "You need to calm down. Be methodical. Think of it like a high-stakes poker game."

Was he kidding?

"Just find the fucking plane or train or whatever the hell this guy is taking her away on."

"It has to be a plane," Liam reasoned. "A train or a car would take too long. If they were willing to hire a hitman to force her, then those assholes are desperate. They won't want to wait."

He paused for a moment. "I should have known something was wrong when Tahlia called you Trick. She never uses your nickname. It's always Patrick with her."

Trick's guts twisted as he remembered the near-hysterical explanation Maggie had given him when she and Peyton came to find him. They'd been hugging the floor, trying to stay out of sight of the windows when Peyton finally clapped her hand over Maggie's mouth to tell him what happened in a clear clipped voice.

Liam's phone chimed, and he texted a rapid reply. "Eric just got there. He's going to sedate Maggie."

"He's *what?*" Jason's shout came through Ethan's phone loud and clear.

"Let him do what he has to do," Liam snapped. "We gotta focus on Tahlia now."

Jason swore. "I know," he apologized. "We've got two possibilities out of a private airfield near Lexington. I think those are our best bet."

Trick swore aloud. They were at the highway split he needed to take to get to Lexington. Gritting his teeth, he shifted gears, cutting a car off to make the lane change in time.

Liam murmured something, but he kept his mouth shut as they sped along. Trick pulled off the highway a few minutes later, gunning the engine until they almost hydroplaned into the lot of the small airfield.

His brother got out of the car first, but he didn't have Trick's motivation. He outran Liam, bursting into the nearest hanger ahead of him by several lengths.

He scanned the space. Two jets were parked there when there

was room for more. A white-haired couple was preparing a small snub-nosed Cessna.

"Where is it?" he shouted at them.

"Where is what?" The wrinkled woman backed away from him, her eyes wide. He must look like a madman.

"The plane from this spot," he said, pointing to the empty space. "If it's the one headed to Florida, I need to stop it from taking off."

The white-haired man put his fingers on his wife's arm. "I'm sorry, young man. That plane took off ten minutes ago."

"No!"

Liam stopped him mid-collapse. Patrick's hands were on his knees as he sucked in hard lungfuls of air.

"We need to follow that plane immediately," Liam said. "How fast is your plane?"

The man held his hands up, shooing them away. "Sorry, son, we're about to leave for the Bahamas. It's our anniversary."

He and his wife turned and began to walk away. Trick straightened, rushing forward to pull the guy back by his collar. "That plane has my whole life on it. My fiancée has been kidnapped. What will it take for you to fly us after it?" he asked, pointing to a sleek jet at the end of the hanger.

"Uh…" The man exchanged a frown with his wife.

"He's serious," Liam said. "We're waiting for a few FBI agents to join us. How does ten thousand dollars sound as recompense? That would pay for a decent anniversary redo, wouldn't it?"

The couple glanced at each other, the husband backing away.

"We're here!" Trick turned to see Jason and Ethan running inside. He turned back to the old couple.

"Twenty thousand."

Silence.

"Fifty."

"Oh, well, I suppose we can talk to Harry about changing our flight plan," the old woman said, poking her husband in his ribs.

"Please do it now."

The old man shrugged, but he frowned as the two agents joined them. "Our plane can't seat all of you. Two extra at the most. Plus, we'll be heavy. That'll slow us down, and it sounds like you are in a rush."

"We can unload the luggage," the wife chimed in.

"Is there another plane and pilot around here?" Jason asked.

"Come with me." The wife hurried out of the hanger. Jason followed her.

Ethan turned to Liam. "You have to stay behind, too. Find another plane and follow us."

His brother scowled. "What? Why?"

"Because I'm the one with the gun."

Liam conceded with bad grace. "We'll be right behind you," he said, then pointed at Patrick. "Don't let this one get his head blown off."

They unloaded the luggage in record time. The old man frowned as his Burberry luggage hit the deck hard, but he didn't complain. They were in the air a few minutes later.

CHAPTER 30

Tahlia distantly registered the sting of the slap across the face. Someone was trying to wake her up, and not gently.

She'd spent the flight trying to bribe Killian, pleading with him not to turn her over to her psycho family. Apparently, that failed. Her last memory was of him coming toward her with a syringe.

Groaning, Tahlia put her hands up to try and block the next blow. Her cousin Dante swore from somewhere above her. "It's about time you woke up, you bitch."

"Why did you wake her?" Uncle Lucas snapped. "It's better if she's out for the ceremony. Get everything ready. I have something to take care of."

His heavy footsteps signaled he was leaving. More grumbled conversation between her cousins followed.

It had grown quiet when she finally cracked her eyelids open. Her arms and legs were tied at the wrist and ankles. She was propped up in an armchair in her father's old office. The desk was gone. So was the carpet. In its place was a pentagram drawn with thick layers of white powder.

Shit.

Her cousin Cain's face filled her field of view as he knelt in front of her. "You thought you could go off and fucking live happily ever after, didn't you?"

His smug face twisted into a sneer. "Well, that was never going to happen. It's not what you were born for. You were fucking bred for one purpose—to serve your family. And no one, not some trumped-up new money hotel owner, or any of your friends, are going to get in the way of that. Dad has fucking cancer for fuck's sake."

She blinked. "How is that my fault?" Her voice was a raspy mess.

Somewhere in the background, her uncle Lucas swore. "Stop talking to the sacrifice and get this incense pot ready."

Tahlia stared at the pentagram, dread pooling in her stomach.

I knew it. She'd denied the truth for so long, she almost convinced herself she didn't know why her family wanted her.

In reality, the knowledge had always been there in the back of her mind. It was why she'd been raised the way she had—like a veal. She was never meant to be a real person, one with independent thoughts or feelings. It was why her father hadn't bothered to have her educated until forced and why he ignored her existence until her stepmother and brother were gone.

According to these psychos, the family's prosperity was tied to the demon they worshipped. And demons required sacrifices. Live human sacrifices.

Why couldn't they use a damn goat?

"Was this how my mother died?" Tahlia asked.

She'd always wondered about the woman who'd given birth to her. This was her last chance to learn the truth.

"As if that dirty bitch was good enough for Mammon," Cain spat. "*He* requires genuine sacrifice—the eldest child of the first-born. That's why your father knocked up a maid. It's a long-standing family tradition. We know better than to get attached to Mammon's gift. Everything would have been fucking fine if your baby brother—the real heir—hadn't died. Unable to have more children, Salvatore turned to you, letting you go off to fucking Harvard for fuck's sake. So now Mammon's sacrifice is *years* late, and it's your fucking fault."

Her mind reeled as the sheer perversity penetrated her mind. Her whole body ached, but the deepest wound was to her heart.

You knew that about him, she reminded herself. Her father's belated pride in her accomplishments came only after he'd lost her brother. He'd turned to her because he had no one else, nothing he could point to with pride.

Her accomplishments in academia had given Salvatore that, but it didn't seem to matter. She wanted to shrivel up and crawl into a hole.

"Are we even sure this is going to work?" Lucas grumbled. "She's not pure anymore."

Ugh. Was it supposed to be a virgin sacrifice?

Wait. That meant she was unsuitable now. *Please God,* Tahlia prayed, but Cain dashed her hopes.

"That part doesn't really matter. Pure is in the eye of the beholder. Mammon will take her. At this point, he must be hungry enough."

Did that mean they thought the demon was going to eat her or…Tahlia wrinkled her nose.

Great. Just perfect. Tahlia pressed her bound wrists against her thighs as the heady incense smoke began to fill the room. The smell of it made her gag even as the room began to spin and her lids grew heavy.

Not again, she thought, recognizing the taint from the time she accidentally walked into Chang's back room. The incense was laced with opium.

Soon, she was listing to one side, her head lolling as she tried to fight off the effects of the drug.

Cain picked her up, handling her like a sack of potatoes. He picked his way through the room, careful not to step on any of the lines of the pentagram as he deposited her in the center. Then he let her alone, trusting the drug to do its work.

CHAPTER 31

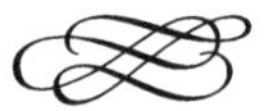

Trick ripped his suit jacket off. He balled it up and shoved it under a bush.

The humid Florida air made his shirt stick to his skin, but the sun was finally starting to dip in the sky.

"Are you sure they're here?" he asked Ethan.

The FBI agent was checking his phone. He was also in his shirt sleeves. "This is where we tracked the car that met the plane."

Trick rubbed his eyes. "It just seems crazy these people would bring her to their home." His hand swept out to encompass the expansive lawn of the Palm Beach estate.

They'd snuck over a tall spiked brick garden wall a few minutes ago. No alarm bells sounded, and they hadn't been met with goons with guns.

Trick was half out of his mind. As soon as he saw the house, he'd started running toward it, but Ethan yanked his collar and dragged him behind a clump of bushes next to a big bald cypress tree.

Ethan scoffed. "You expect *sane* from these people?"

He had a point. "All right then. What are we waiting for?"

"Back up," Ethan said, checking the latest message on his phone. "*Fuck*. We have our warrant, but the local bureau office is only now mobilizing. They're at least a half hour out."

That was too long. "We can't wait."

He could feel it in his gut. They needed to get to Tahlia now.

"I agree," Ethan said, surprising him. It must have shown on his face because the agent snorted at him impatiently. "They're lunatics who worship the devil. We don't know what they are doing to her."

Trick flinched, but Ethan just frowned, pointing out a guard patrolling near the house. "Don't think about it. We go when he rounds the corner."

He nodded. "Why aren't there more of them?"

These people were obviously wealthy. They had a private beach for fuck's sake. He'd expected the place to be crawling with armed guards.

"More guards, more witnesses." Ethan never pulled his punches. The agent peeked around the tree. "Okay, go now!"

He started running, following the other man as he sprinted to the massive old-world-style mansion. They ran along the left wing of the house, crouching beneath a darkened window.

It was empty. "We should split up," he said in a low voice as Ethan lifted the sash.

The agent climbed inside. "No way. I only have my service piece. What if you run into someone with a gun?"

"I don't know how to shoot anyway." He dropped into the room lightly after Ethan.

It was a salon of some kind. He landed next to a turn-of-the-century fainting couch. Expensive antiques littered the room.

"All the more reason we should stick together."

"Fine," he growled, reluctantly letting Ethan take the lead. Together, they prowled the hallway, peeking into room after empty room.

How big was this damn place? He shuddered to think of the twisted childhood Tahlia had under this roof.

They turned the corner, finding themselves in a luxuriously appointed foyer. An imposing mahogany staircase descended from a second story. Twin hallways swept into darkened recesses on either side.

"Which one first?" he asked.

Ethan opened his mouth to answer when a dark-suited man stepped out of the shadowy left hallway. "Sir, I think we have intruders. A motion sensor near the wall was trip—"

The security guard glanced up in time to meet Ethan's fist with his nose. Unfortunately, the stranger must have been on steroids or something. Physically, he was near Ethan's build. The sucker punch didn't take him down.

Ethan and the man grappled. "I got this. Go find Tahlia," Ethan grunted as he punched the man again.

Trick didn't need to be told twice. He whirled around. Which hallway?

Damn, I need some of Tahlia's luck.

Unbidden, an image of him slipping his engagement ring onto Tahlia's hand flashed through his mind.

Left. Go left.

THE LOCKED double doors wouldn't budge. That was how he knew he'd found the right place. His instincts were screaming. Tahlia needed him.

Trick reared back and kicked with all his might. The door splintered, but the wood was too thick. Focusing, he put everything he had into the rapid strikes. It took three more blows before the door fell open.

He plunged into the room, his eyes watering as a thin acrid

smoke hit his face. Inside was a nightmare straight out of a B-level horror movie.

He'd found her, but Tahlia was gagged and bound. She was lying motionless in the middle of a white powdery pentagram surrounded by candles and strange occult symbols. His dramatic entrance interrupted a chant from a robed man at the upper left point of the star.

Putting his hands up, he registered motion from his left. Someone rushed him, hitting him in the middle.

But Trick was ready. He twisted, blocking the guy's tackle. Years of no-holds-barred wrestling and sparring with his brother honed his reaction time to a sharp-steeled edge.

He followed the block with a lightning-fast punch. It glanced off the guy's head, but it slowed him down enough for him to get a second shot in. The guy hit the floor, sliding against Trick's leg.

"Patrick?" Tahlia moaned and turned, rolling on the floor to face him.

Relief flooded through him as her eyes opened, but she couldn't seem to focus on him. She blinked, her mouth gaping.

He swayed, wanting to run to her. The other man in the room was coming around, being careful to step around the pentagram.

That was when things got weird.

Trick's vision blurred, and he swayed on his feet. Objects in the room began to glow with an iridescent edge. The second man tackled him while he was distracted by a sparkling blue table.

He hit the floor with a grunt, fighting back with lackluster coordination.

What the fuck was wrong with this room? His limbs were growing heavier, and everything was waving or blinking at him. Trick was a skilled fighter, but he'd never done it while under the influence.

Doesn't matter. He needed to get it together. Tahlia's life was at stake.

A fist landed in his gut, nearly incapacitating him. His abs absorbed the shock, but the pain cleared some of the haze in his head. Giving himself a shake, he clamped his hands on the guy's head, boxing his ears before twisting them.

The man's scream was deafening. He reared back, giving Trick room to punch him. He followed that with a kick that knocked the second man next into the first. Both groaned as one landed on top of the other.

"Only one can pass," a new voice said.

Trick blinked, searching for a third assailant, but his head was spinning too fast. He put his hands on his head, trying to steady his vision.

"Patrick." It was barely a whisper.

Tahlia.

He forgot about everything else. She was there, at his feet. Bound hand and foot, she'd managed to crawl toward him from the center of the pentagram, breaking the circle of white powder surrounding it.

"No!" one of the men screamed, hitting a frequency that made Trick's ears ring.

Out of nowhere, a roar filled the room. Wincing, he got down on his hands and knees, pulling Tahlia toward him.

More screaming followed. Trick's head was pounding. His vision was starting to fade in and out, and he couldn't figure out what the hell was going on. The only solid thing was Tahlia in his arms. She was counting on him. Unable to pull her behind him, he crawled in front of her to shield her.

"What have you done?" someone shouted.

One of the robed men was shrieking, his mouth fixed wide like a berserker. He was holding a knife.

The double doors burst open. He distantly registered a bang and a thud. Then everything went dark.

"WAKE UP, PRINCESS."

He opened his eyes to see Ethan standing over him with a bag. Trick examined his surroundings, sitting up slowly when his head swam. He was on a gurney in the back of a van. An ambulance to be more precise.

"Where's Tahlia? Where am I?"

Ethan leaned against the ambulance door. "You're in hell house's driveway," he answered. "And don't worry. Tahlia's fine. She's in another ambulance. You've been out for over an hour. The coroner is here. He's started picking up the pieces."

What the hell did that mean? Trick unclipped the belt.

Ethan waved him back down. "The paramedics said you shouldn't move."

"Fuck that." He staggered to his feet, hopping unsteadily.

She was only a few feet away. Tahlia had eschewed the gurney, too. She was sitting on the rear bumper of her ambulance while a paramedic took her vitals.

She turned, her eyes lighting up when she saw him. "What happened?"

He joined her on the bumper, throwing an arm around her shoulders. "That's what I would like to know."

They both turned to Ethan. The agent put his hands and his hips. "Basically, everyone's dead and you're both recovering from an opium overdose."

"Shit," he muttered. It felt as if his head was stuffed with cotton wool and his tongue was dry. *I need water.*

Ethan gestured back to the house with his thumb. "Those were some seriously crazy fuckers."

"Were?" Tahlia asked, blinking dazedly. She must have missed his earlier statement.

"Yeah. Both are dead. We're rounding up the guards. Apparently, all but the head of security had been ordered to keep clear of the house."

Tahlia's brow creased. "By both do you mean my cousins Dante and Cain?"

"Um, probably." Ethan shrugged. "Two guys in their twenties. They didn't exactly have I.D. on them." He pursed his lips. "And one of them didn't have a head..." He turned to Trick. "I don't suppose you did that?"

Trick stared at him openmouthed. He was speechless.

Ethan sighed. "Yeah, I didn't think so. Not enough blood on you. Which means twin two did it. Now, he's got plenty of blood on him, but that's mostly because I shot him. He was coming at you with a knife."

"Oh." Tahlia gripped his hand. She looked as confused as he felt. "What about my uncle Lucas? I was kind of out of it when I woke up here, but he was in the room. He didn't stay, though. After that, I lost track of...well, everything."

"That would have been the incense. I got a blast of it, too, when the door opened. It nearly knocked me on my ass. I needed to open the window just to see straight. I can't believe those two psycho cousins of yours could even walk in there, but they did have some weird cowl-mask thing over their mouths. Still...that shit was fucked up."

He reached over to pat Tahlia on the shoulder. "I don't think you have to worry about those a-holes anymore."

"Except for Uncle Lucas," she pointed out.

"We'll find him," Ethan assured her. "I've got local agents scouring the place. And Jason and Liam are ten minutes out."

An agent wearing one of those blue windbreakers with the yellow letters hailed him from the door of the mansion. They met halfway up the drive and had a hurried convo.

Ethan jogged back to them. "Tahlia, do you have the code for the panic room?"

She stared at him blankly. "There's a panic room? Where is it?"

"It's behind the library, in the room next to your father's office. I think your uncle is hiding there. We've searched everywhere else, and the garage is full. Every car registered to this address is there."

Trick squeezed Tahlia, pressing her closer to him. Once they were done here, he was going to burn this place to the ground.

"I'm sure the code is written down somewhere. Or we can guess it," he said, rubbing Tahlia's back. "She's pretty good with numbers."

Ethan smiled. "We can try that. Just stay out of creep central, aka your father's office."

They followed him inside, giving the office a wide berth.

The library was crowded. One shelf was on hinges. It was pulled away from the wall, exposing a thick steel door with a dated electronic keypad.

"The shelf was open a crack," Ethan said. "That's the only reason we found it so soon."

A technician was standing in front of the keypad while a few agents poked around the library, searching for papers with the code.

Eventually, they asked Tahlia for help.

"Don't worry if you can't guess it," Ethan told her before taking out his service piece. "But if you can and he's in there, we're ready."

Tahlia glanced at him. "I can't believe this has been here the whole time."

"At least ten years," Ethan confirmed.

"So my father put it in. Maybe it's his birthday." She leaned over the technician and punched in a series of numbers. It buzzed negatively. She tried a few more combinations, none of which worked either.

"Maybe it's your birthday," Trick suggested.

Tahlia rolled her eyes, her lips turned down, but she put in the numbers anyway. A green LED lit, and the door swung open with a click.

Trick pulled Tahlia behind him. Another agent pulled out their weapon. He and Ethan nodded at each other, before they yanked the door wide, their guns drawn.

"What the fuck is this?" Ethan snapped, putting away his gun. He and the backup agent stepped inside, lowering their weapons.

Once they moved, Trick saw Lucas—or what was left of him.

A florid middle-aged man sat in an office chair behind a small mahogany desk, head still attached to his body. But he was dead, the cause the large bullet hole in the middle of this forehead.

The corpse was holding a pen as if he were writing a letter. There was a piece of paper in front of him.

Behind him, Tahlia gasped. He turned in time to see her hands fly to her mouth.

"Uncle Lucas!"

He wrapped his arms around her. "Don't look baby."

"Who shot him?" she asked, throwing her hands up to cover her face.

Ethan walked out of the panic room, holding the paper from the desk. "I think this may explain that. Who's Killian?"

"What?" Tahlia raised her head and snatched the sheet from his hands. Trick read over her shoulder.

TAHLIA,

Forgive me for taking my leave before the authorities arrived. After you protested your innocence so succinctly, I decided to study your father's death in greater detail. I soon learned Lucas hired me under false pretenses, so I decided to take care of him for you. Consider it an early wedding present. Also, he refused to pay me.

Kindest Regards,

Killian

TRICK HELD Tahlia's hand as the authorities wrapped up. All the bodies—and the pieces of bodies—had been carted away by the authorities.

Ethan and the other agents took his statement twice. They'd wanted to talk to Tahlia alone to take hers, but he put his foot down. He refused to let her out his sight...at least until she excused herself to go to the bathroom.

Liam was in deep discussion with their family's lawyers despite the fact Ethan assured them no charges would be filed against them. But Liam wasn't taking any chances. He'd seen the headless corpse of Tahlia's cousin and called the cavalry in.

Meanwhile, Trick was waiting in the hall with his hands in his pockets He wanted nothing more than to leave this place, but Jason had a point. They needed to dot their I's and cross their T's so they would never have to come back here again.

The door to the office was open a crack. Unable to resist, he walked over to it, checking for stray agents before slipping inside.

It was safe to breathe in there now. Ethan had opened the windows and doused the incense burners right after he'd shot Cain.

The agents had been busy. Little yellow flags surrounded the partially demolished pentagram and the various pools of blood. The biggest of those was right next to the break in the line Tahlia made when she'd crawled toward him.

A little dizzy, Trick covered his eyes and spun around. He opened his eyes to see himself. There was a large antique mirror hanging next to the door.

Trick stared at his own reflection. There were a million thoughts running through his head, but he couldn't grab hold of one long enough to examine it. It was as if the part of his mind capable of reason and logic was wrapped in a thick layer of spun wool.

Movement in the mirror caught his eye. He swiveled, but no one was there.

Trick's reflection grinned at him. Startled, he blinked and rubbed his eyes.

His stomach twisted, and a cold chill ran down his spine.

"This is crazy," he muttered.

His reflection didn't follow suit. It just kept grinning.

Trick pointed a shaky finger at the mirror. "You can't have her," he hissed. "*She's mine.*"

The demon in the mirror smiled at him. It did a little gesture with its hand as if to say *we'll see*.

"Patrick?"

Trick jumped about a foot. In the mirror, his reflection did, too.

Tahlia was peeking around the door, her eyes studiously avoiding the bloodstains in front of her. "Ethan says we can leave now."

He almost ran toward her. Her eyes widened as he hugged her to him, squeezing far too hard. He pulled her away from the door, dragging her away from that foul room as fast as her feet could carry her.

"Let's get the hell out of here," he said, throwing open the front door.

His heart didn't stop racing until they were all the way down the drive on their way to the airport.

CHAPTER 32

Tahlia leaned against the back of the sofa, wrapping her arms around Patrick's neck from behind.

They were in his office at the Caislean, sharing a lunch with Ethan as the latter went over the bureau's official findings on what happened at her family's estate in Florida.

"Of course you were hallucinating," Ethan said. "Do you know how much opium smoke you inhaled?"

He waved the folder at them before dropping it to finish plowing through the Caislean's signature tri-tip sandwich.

Patrick's sandwich sat untouched in front of him.

She rubbed his shoulders. "Don't make me feed you by hand," she teased before coming around to sit next to him. "You've lost too much weight since we got back from Florida."

He sighed and snaked a hand around her waist. "I'm not hungry. Why don't you have some? You finished yours so quickly."

Tahlia blushed. It was true. She'd been starving lately. And sometimes, she still got dizzy. It happened often enough she'd asked the hotel's concierge doctor for a checkup. Given the number of times she'd been drugged with unknown substances, he'd been concerned enough to conduct a battery of tests. She was meeting him soon to get the results.

Tahlia refused to be afraid. Whatever was going on with her physically was a blip compared to what she'd been through. Her uncle and cousins were gone. She was finally free, and nothing was going to stop her from getting her happily ever after.

"Trick, you have to get over this thing. You were *high*," Ethan said in between bites.

Always a big eater, he was starting to eye Patrick's untouched meal. Tahlia nabbed it before he could claim it.

"I know what I saw."

"I'm not saying you didn't see it. I did shrooms once. I saw lots of weird shit, too. But none of it was real."

Tahlia sighed and kept eating. This was an old argument with Ethan. He kept bringing up the hallucination. Her soon-to-be husband didn't like to talk about it. It took a few weeks for him to even tell her about it. In fact, she'd been forced to threaten breaking off the engagement before he finally told her about his experience.

Ethan nudged the report across the coffee table. "This is your copy of the bureau's final report. They're pretty interested in this Killian character. They were able to match the bullet in your uncle to two other high-profile deaths, and he's suspected in dozens more."

She shifted in her seat uncomfortably and put the sandwich down. Wiping her hands, she leaned closer to Patrick.

"I'm not surprised. He seemed so calm and controlled the whole time. The only thing that got his attention was when I told him how my dad really died. I guess it was shocking enough for a facilitator, or whatever he wanted to call himself, to sit up and take notice."

"Facilitator, my ass. He's a contract killer who does a little transporting on the side for the right price." Patrick rubbed her back before putting a possessive hand around her waist. "We're lucky he left you alone after double-crossing your uncle—although I hate the idea of someone like this even knowing your name, let alone doing you a favor."

Ethan tsked and shook his head. "That's not it. If Lucas thought he could get away with not paying someone like that, he was crazier than I thought. If this guy is who we think he is, then he's been responsible for regime-changing assassinations. I honestly don't know why he would do something like this. It must have been small potatoes compared to his usual jobs."

Tahlia opened the report to the sketch they'd made of the man who called himself Killian. It wasn't a perfect likeness, but she supposed it was close enough.

"What if he comes after me because I can recognize him? I bet the only reason he let me see his face was because he thought I was going to die."

Patrick frowned, his face pale, but Ethan just shrugged. "If he was going to kill you, he would have done it before he left the estate. My guess is he wore some prosthetics to change his appearance—nothing major, just enough to make it hard to identify him later. Kind of like we did for Trick that one time."

"When was that?" Tahlia twisted to look at Patrick. He'd never mentioned wearing prosthetic makeup.

"It's a long story," he told her. He turned to Ethan. "Are you sure about this? It says here Killian decapitated the cousin, too."

"Well, it wasn't either of you," Ethan grumbled. "For one, the blood splatter on your clothes didn't match. And you'd probably faint if you got one of those tailored shirts that dirty."

Patrick glared at the agent. "Fuck you."

"Whenever I'm at loose ends, I'll think of you first," Ethan promised before gesturing at Tahlia. "But this one might object… unless, of course, you guys decide to spice things up with a threes—"

Ethan was hit simultaneously. Patrick's pillow hit him on the left side of his head and hers on the right. Ethan shut his mouth after that, but the wicked grin he threw her might have done some damage if she wasn't madly in love with someone else.

Patrick picked at the salad garnish on his plate. "I still don't think this Killian character killed the cousin. He would have used a gun like he did on the uncle."

Personally, Tahlia agreed, but so many things about that day were a mess in her mind. She couldn't be sure what really happened. She might never know.

Ethan sniffed. "If I wasn't him, then it was the other cousin—the one I shot. Because there was no trace of anyone else in that room."

Patrick opened his mouth as if he wanted to say something, but he pressed his lips shut. "Yeah, I know. Anyone else would have been passed out on the floor. You needed a gas mask in that room."

"My point exactly. You had a drug-fueled delusion. Happens to the best of us. As for the freak cousins, maybe they were used to that stuff—up to a point. Some people build up a tolerance, but it's possible they overestimated in their rush to conduct their ritual."

That sounded plausible to Tahlia. Killian certainly hadn't killed her father, and she didn't think there were two killers running around cutting people's heads off in this affair.

Patrick looked unconvinced, but he gave her a bracing smile. She checked her watch.

Shoot. It was almost time for her appointment with the doctor.

"What about the rest of the relatives?" she asked. "Have any of them come forward to accuse me of somehow orchestrating these deaths, too?"

"Nope. No one has made a peep about that. I was, however, contacted by that asshole law firm in Manhattan. Unfortunately, your uncle Lucas inherited your father's estate, at least according to them. And you are specifically excluded from Lucas' will. I'm afraid you don't get a share of the family fortune."

He cleared his throat and straightened as if bracing himself. "Also, when the agents gave them the opportunity, none of them wanted to send a message to you."

There was a tiny tremor in her lip. "So it's official. I don't have a family."

She held up her hands. "Doesn't matter. I don't want that lot either. And I definitely don't want any of that money. They can keep the house, too, and everything in it. It can go to whatever relative wants it. As long as they don't ever contact me again, they are welcome to it."

"Are you sure about that?" Ethan asked. "It's a buttload of money. You could always fight the will in court. Any jury with a half a brain cell to share between them would side with you."

Tahlia shook her head vehemently. "Not a penny."

"She doesn't need their money." Patrick was just as adamant. "And you do have family. You have me."

Ethan shrugged as Tahlia sighed and cuddled closer to her fiancé. "If you insist. Seems a pity. It would really stick it to them if you sued for the cash. But if Trick wants to do the what's-mine-is yours-thing after you get married, more power to you. It's not like he can't afford it."

Tahlia's smile was smug. "Patrick knows I don't need his money. And if I do someday, I'll win it off him fair and square."

Both men laughed, and she stood with a decent approximation of regret. "I have to run. I'm meeting the girls for coffee," she lied.

Tahlia hadn't told Patrick about her doctor's appointment. She didn't want to needlessly worry him.

"Oh...I could use a cup before I drive back." Ethan jumped up.

Damn it. She should have said something else. Ethan was always ready for an excuse to see Peyton. "Sorry, it's going to be the final reveal of my wedding dress. Girls only."

Ethan wasn't deterred. "Isn't it only bad luck if it's the groom? I promise I won't tell anyone what it looks like."

Trick stood and clapped him on the shoulder.

"Let the ladies do their thing. How can they talk about us if we're there?" He walked over to the bar. "Come on. I'll make you a coffee from the pod machine here."

Ethan followed him and she snuck out of the room, hurrying down to the hotel's medical office.

TAHLIA STARED AT ERIC TAM, the head of the concierge medical team that worked for the hotel.

"I'm what?"

"Pregnant." He glanced at his chart. "And quite a bit farther along than I would have guessed looking at you. But there is some firmness in your stomach now. I'm guessing you're not going to show until you pop."

Tahlia's hand flew to her middle. It was true. Her stomach was harder than she remembered.

"But I haven't been sick." She hadn't experienced any nausea… just a little dizziness.

Oh, crap.

"Have your breasts been more sensitive than normal?"

Her eyes flew up to meet Dr. Tam's. "Maybe a little." Her blush was a fiery red.

"What about the baby?" she asked, her stomach fluttering. "Is it okay? Will the drugs I was given affect it?"

"My educated guess would be no, but technically there is a risk. I'm more concerned with the opium smoke you were exposed to, although honestly, Trick had more in his system. Since you were on the ground most of the time, you escaped getting the bulk of the effect. Trick breathed in more because he was standing and fighting, exerting himself."

He leaned forward. "I can't say with certainty there will be no adverse effects to the baby, but I have seen infants born under far more difficult circumstances. Children of drug addicts or women undergoing treatment for cancer or on anti-psychotic medication for example. Some of those children did have problems in the beginning, but most of them went on to have happy and productive lives with a little TLC."

Dr. Tam patted her hand. "You and Patrick are both very healthy. We'll monitor this pregnancy closely, but I predict you're going to get lucky and everything will be fine."

Tahlia inhaled deeply, calming down instantly. "You're right. We are lucky." She got up and thanked him, promising to tell Patrick right away so they could set up their first joint sonogram.

PATRICK SPUN AROUND. Tahlia was standing there over the remains of their gourmet meal, her hands twisting around the napkin.

"Pregnant?"

She rose from the small dining table. They were supposed to eat with his brother and Caroline, but Tahlia had asked him to reschedule. He'd done so gladly, thinking she wanted some alone time before the wedding or—and this was ungenerous of him—to spare him a night of Caroline's company. She knew he wasn't a big fan of his brother's girlfriend.

This news was the last thing he expected.

Tahlia's hands went to her stomach, her big blue eyes fixed on his face. "I realize this isn't how you wanted to start our marriage. I'd thought we'd wait a few years before we talked about having kids. And Dr. Tam acknowledged there *is* a risk to the baby given the stuff that's happened. He wants to monitor us closely."

He stared at her hands. They were folded over her stomach protectively.

"Only one can pass," he said, blinking down at her.

Her brow creased in confusion before she wrinkled her nose. She threw the napkin at him. "Don't even think of suggesting I was rejected as an offering to a demon because I was pregnant."

Trick deserved every bit of her scorn, but he couldn't stop his mind from racing. *That's why they wanted to keep her a virgin.* It didn't have anything to do with her purity. It was because whatever doorway they were opening was only meant for one. *Two couldn't pass.*

He stayed quiet too long. Tahlia's eyes flashed like liquid silver. "Damn it, Patrick. It wasn't real. And *it's over.*"

He blinked. *She's right.* And so was Ethan. He couldn't continue to harp on that day in Florida. If he did, he was going to go mad. He couldn't even look in the mirror. Thankfully, no one noticed.

"I'm going to be a father." Suddenly, everything brightened. He could see every object in the room with startling sharpness and clarity. Tahlia and the baby needed him.

He rushed forward, sweeping her into his arms and squeezing her tight. "Our baby is a miracle, and he or she is going to be perfect."

Tahlia's head dropped forward, hitting him in the chest as she let herself relax. "Don't scare me like that. I thought you were losing it."

Trick shook his head. Maybe he was right and it *was* what the voice meant, but it didn't matter anymore. He was going to go back to his life, the one he'd planned for himself the moment he met Tahlia.

Well, going to church a little more often can't hurt...

He took Tahlia's hand, intending on pulling her to their bed, but she pushed him, propelling him into the smaller room on the left before she started to undo his tie.

He didn't understand what was going on until she reached down to undo his pants.

"You want to have sex in my *closet?*"

"No, I want to make love here," she said, turning to flip the interior doors closed. She moved a few of the coat racks he'd strategically placed in front of the mirrors built into the wall. When they were gone, the semicircular alcove at the mouth of his walk-in closet reflected their images back at them four-fold.

Aw, hell. She had noticed.

He tried to play it off. "Wouldn't you be more comfortable in bed?"

She replied by taking off her blouse.

One glimpse of her creamy skin pressed against the blue lace bra and he was done arguing.

"Here's fine." Trick hastily pulled at his jacket and shirt, stripping down to his boxers in a flash.

He was faster than she was. She was still wearing her knee-length wool skirt when he pushed his shorts down.

Being surrounded by reflections of himself didn't matter. He only had eyes for her. Up until she turned her back, bracing her hands on the mirror on the right, the one bolted to the wall.

Her silver-blue eyes flashed over her shoulder, challenging him.

If he hadn't already been in love with her before, he would have dropped to his knees right then.

It was such good idea, he did it anyway, kneeling behind her, holding her hips against his face. He reached up to unzip her skirt, dragging it down with his hands.

Trick pressed his lips to the edge of her satin and lace panties. It was part of a matching set, but she was going to have to wear a different pair with that bra from now on.

He took hold of the fabric high on her hip, twisting the delicate cloth until it tore. She gasped, turning to look down at him. The other side tore just as easily. By the time he pulled the shredded fabric away, she was so wet her lips glistened for him.

Trick kissed the bare skin of her hip and rear, his hand moving up the silk of her inner thigh until he was there, her velvet slit so hot it almost scalded his fingers.

Tahlia moaned and leaned back into his hand, trying to increase the pressure. But he didn't oblige. He urged her forward until she was bent nearly ninety degrees, bracing herself with her arms. His mouth went to her pussy, feasting. His tongue lapped, his teeth grazing her sensitive folds as she panted, calling his name.

She writhed against him, forcing him to hold her fast against his mouth.

Her taste was indescribable, familiar yet subtly different. Could that be the pregnancy?

He didn't know and didn't care. Tahlia was his goddess, and he was going to worship all night.

"Come inside me." Tahlia wiggled her hips, trying to urge him up. Trick rose, staring at her face in the mirror. He moved, wrapping his arms under her breasts, holding her chin with his hand.

His cock drove home in one long, slow thrust as she continued to brace herself against the mirror. It was agonizing and simultaneously the most intense pleasure he'd ever felt. Throwing his head back, he savored Tahlia's heated tightness.

She fit him like a glove. "You are the hottest, sweetest thing I've ever felt," he whispered, penetrating as deep as he could, the tip of his cock touching her womb.

He couldn't avoid the mirror. Trick wanted to see Tahlia's face as he fucked her. She knew that, of course. She knew him too well —what he thought and liked to do. Most of the time, she knew what he was going to say before he said it. And in bed…

It was the kind of connection poets wrote about—hot, dirty, sensual, and sacred all at the same time.

Before Tahlia, he hadn't spared much thought to love, not the kind that lasted more than a night or two. He'd had it easy.

Easy was crap. Compared to this, every relationship he'd had was a pale tasteless imitation.

"Shit, Tahl..." This time, it was him moaning as she tightened and flexed around him. Instinct took over. He kept her pinned against him, his hand holding her head by the chin as he thrust harder and harder.

The smooth taut skin of her backside rubbed against him as he pumped, grinding against her until he found her G-spot. A few determined strokes later and she was shivering, her whole body tensing before she clamped down, her orgasm sweeping over her like a violent wind.

Tahlia's mouth gaped, and her hands slid down the mirror as her strength failed. He held her with one arm and used the other to brace himself for one more desperate minute, his hips pistoning irregularly as his rhythm broke down. Another stroke and he exploded. Holding her fast against him, he watched himself pour everything he had into her.

He used the last of his strength to coordinate their fall. They slid down the wall together. His heat warmed the mirror as he sat leaning against it, cradling Tahlia's naked body against him.

"I don't think I'm going to be able to look in any of these mirrors without getting a hard-on."

Tahlia giggled, her hand languidly sliding up to caress his cheek.

"Don't get mad at me for asking this..."

He smiled down at her. Her expression was serious, but there was teasing glint in her eye.

"What is it?"

She waved at the mirrors. "Do you think that exorcised your demons?"

He laughed aloud, catching sight of their reflection—her

golden body cradled in his. He'd never seen anything more beautiful.

Tahlia was a gift. Their connection was bigger and more precious than love, and soon, they were going to be a family of three. One crazy experience wouldn't stop him from taking care of them.

He met Tahlia's eyes in the mirror. "Definitely."

EPILOGUE

Patrick Tyler joined Tahlia Maria Delavordo in wedded bliss three days after his twenty-ninth birthday—breaking the hearts of thousands of single women in the process. At least that was what the tabloids said about it. The only person who cared about the headlines was the hotel's publicist.

The wedding at the Caislean Boston was a small and intimate affair. Flowers decked the small conference room, which had been transformed by Maggie and the staff into the most glorious chapel. Instead of being married by a justice of the peace, Patrick opted for a priest from the local Catholic archdiocese.

The makeshift chapel was the very same room where they'd held that awful memorial service for Tahlia. Patrick chose it specifically for that reason. He didn't want either of them to associate any of the rooms of the hotel with bad memories.

They only invited close friends. As for family, only the groom's was in attendance…with one exception. And that extra guest ended up being more than either of them bargained for.

Sometime after the I do's and the whirlwind of photos and

well-wishes from their friends, Patrick motioned to someone in the back of the conference room. A few minutes later, he pulled Tahlia away from Maia and Peyton's effusive congratulations for a surprise.

"I wanted to do this before the ceremony, but flights from Cuba have been a mess since the storm," he said as he led her down one of the lesser-traveled service hallways near the chapel. "It hampered my search. I'd almost given up on trying to find her."

"Find who?"

He answered by opening the door to one of the hotel's private sitting rooms. Sitting on the couch in all her white-haired glory was her Ama, the housekeeper who raised her.

Tahlia burst into tears. She turned to Patrick, hitting him with the bouquet. "How could you not warn me?" she choked out between sobs.

"I'm sorry. I didn't know she was coming until the last minute," he said, stroking her back as he guided her to the couch, which she couldn't see for the tears. "I'm afraid she can't speak much—she had a partial stroke last year, but she still understands everyone just fine."

Her Ama cackled and held out her arms. She leaned over, hugging Tahlia tight to her expansive bosom.

The little old woman was accompanied by a dark-skinned girl, a teenager around fourteen who appeared almost as excited to see her as her Ama.

"Hello, Tahlia, I am cousin Mariposa."

Tahlia raised her head and blinked. "I'm sorry, what did you say?"

Patrick knelt in front of her. "This is the big news—and I swear I didn't know until they got here. See...your dad told you the truth about some things. Your mom did pass away when you were born, but there's a lot he left out."

He put his arm on Ama's shoulder. "What he neglected to mention was that your mother was a member of his domestic staff —as was her mother."

Tahlia's lips parted, and fresh tears stung her eyes. "My Ama is my grandmother?"

Ama took her hand and patted it, making soothing sounds. Both she and Patrick nodded.

"She wasn't allowed to say anything while your father and uncle were alive. They made sure she would never tell you the truth—but they're gone now. And before she went to work for your family, she raised her own back in Cuba. Only her youngest daughter, your mother Anna, joined her in the States. You have two aunts and an uncle in Santa Clara."

Mariposa waved again. "Hi, sorry for my English. I watch some English shows on my computer. My mother is your aunt Juanita."

Patrick smiled. "You have over a dozen cousins. They all wanted to come to the wedding, but some of them couldn't get away yet. There was a lot of storm damage to their neighborhood, but thankfully, all of them are okay. We're floating them a little loan from our many cash wedding gifts by the way. Just a little something to help them rebuild."

She wiped her cheeks. "Thank you. This is the best wedding present I could have asked for."

Ama caressed her check, pressing her forehead to Tahlia's to signal without words how happy she was. They visited a little longer, and then she and Mariposa joined them for the extravagant casino-themed reception.

Hours later, they were dancing in the ballroom. Tahlia whirled in his arms, forgetting all about looking graceful during their dance. Patrick pressed her tight against him, too close for a proper waltz.

"I told you it would be a June wedding," he whispered.

She laughed. “That’s right, you did.” Throwing her arms around him, she kissed him deeply. Cheers erupted from their audience.

Patrick pulled back, his eyes brilliant. “I’m going to love you forever, Mrs. Tyler. And you’re going to love me.”

Tahlia squeezed him tight. “You can bet on it.”

THE END

Finish the Singular Obsession series with the explosive last installment!

"After completing Peyton's Price, I was at a loss for words. The author proved to be quite masterful at creating imagery and evoking reactions." - ***Shannon Winings for Readers' Favorite*** ☆☆☆☆☆

Peyton Carson has been in love with Liam Tyler since she was nine-years-old. All she has ever wanted is for him to see her as something more than just his sister's best friend. But when he gets engaged to someone else, Peyton is devastated. Shattered, she does her best to pick up the pieces and move on with her life. She begins to build a life without Liam in it. But when her roommate's debt becomes her problem, she finds herself in a game too dangerous to play.

Suddenly thrown into unimaginable danger, Peyton has no way out. Unable to rescue her himself, Liam asks for help from the last man he wants anything to do with—Matthias Raske. Now, Peyton's options become clear, but her salvation comes at a price she's not sure she's willing to pay. Peyton must risk it all for a chance at something she's always wanted. Torn between ecstasy and the fairytale, will she overcome all the obstacles or lose her chance at forever?

Available Now

AFTERWORD

Thank you for reading this novel! Reviews are an author's bread and butter. If you liked the story please consider leaving one.

Subscribe to either of my newsletters for a *free* novel!
www.authorlucyleroux.com/newsletter
or keep up with her L.B. Gilbert releases
www.elementalauthor.com/newsletter

ABOUT THE AUTHOR

Lucy Leroux is another name for USA Today Bestselling Author L.B. Gilbert.

Seven years ago Lucy moved to France for a one-year research contract. Six months later she was living with a handsome Frenchman and is now married with an adorable half-french toddler.

When her last contract ended Lucy turned to writing. Frustrated by the lack of quality romance erotica she created her own.

Cursed is the first of many regency novels. Additionally, she writes a bestselling contemporary series. The 'Singular Obsession' books are a combination of steamy romance and suspense that feature intertwining characters in their own stand-alone stories. Follow her on twitter or facebook, or check our her website for more news!

www.authorlucyleroux.com

OTHER BOOKS BY LUCY LEROUX

CODENAME ROMEO

Rogues and Rescuers, Book One

One FBI agent... one single mother... and a toddler who steals his heart.

All FBI agent Ethan Thomas wants is to come home to his new apartment and enjoy the luxury of his new flat-screen TV and some frozen pizza. Encountering a tiny toddler alone in the hall changes everything for the rough and rugged agent. Relief sets in when the child's mother appears. But when she collapses at his feet just before a blizzard hits Boston, Ethan is in over his head.

Now, Ethan is changing diapers and playing doctor… and loving every minute of it. The mother and child need a place to stay, and Ethan can't possibly turn them away. But this investigator knows people—and the woman he's falling for is keeping secrets. Can he uncover the truth while protecting them from the dangers of his job?

Read on Kindle Unlimited

Printed in Great Britain
by Amazon